D0387809

calico
girl

JERDINE NOLEN

A Paula Wiseman Book
Simon & Schuster Books for Young Readers
NEW YORK   LONDON   TORONTO   SYDNEY   NEW DELHI

SIMON & SCHUSTER BOOKS FOR YOUNG READERS
An imprint of Simon & Schuster Children's Publishing Division
1230 Avenue of the Americas, New York, New York 10020
This book is a work of fiction. Any references to historical events, real people, or real
places are used fictitiously. Other names, characters, places, and events are products
of the author's imagination, and any resemblance to actual events or places or persons,
living or dead, is entirely coincidental.
Text copyright © 2017 by Jerdine Nolen
Jacket illustration copyright © 2017 by Sarah Gibb
All rights reserved, including the right of reproduction in whole or in part in any form.
SIMON & SCHUSTER BOOKS FOR YOUNG READERS
is a trademark of Simon & Schuster, Inc.
For information about special discounts for bulk purchases, please contact
Simon & Schuster Special Sales at 1-866-506-1949 or business@simonandschuster.com.
The Simon & Schuster Speakers Bureau can bring authors to your live event.
For more information or to book an event, contact the
Simon & Schuster Speakers Bureau at 1-866-248-3049 or visit our website at
www.simonspeakers.com.
Jacket design by Krista Vossen
Interior design by Hilary Zarycky
The text for this book was set in Bodoni Std.
Manufactured in the United States of America
0117 FFG
First Edition
2 4 6 8 10 9 7 5 3 1
CIP data for this book is available from the Library of Congress.
ISBN 978-1-4814-5981-5
ISBN 978-1-4814-5983-9 (eBook)

To my paternal grandmother, Katie Nolen

CONTENTS

AUTHOR'S NOTE

Maybe growing up in a family where we were not allowed to talk about slavery is the reason, for now, that is all I want, to talk or write about. I have no other explanation than that. I just want to talk about it, know about it, and think about it. It is a very big story. It is as big as the Greek myths we read. And of course, the myths were written as stories to teach about how to live your life. Why couldn't talking about slavery be like that, I wondered? But when I'd asked my father, "Tell me something about what happened during slavery times," his eyes looked fierce, his nostrils flared, and his baritone voice boomed, "In this house, there are *some things* we just aren't going to talk about! No sir, there are some things we just won't discuss." That was that!

It was one of the words that I added to the List of Big Bad Words—most were four-lettered words we were not allowed to say. I confess I did defy my father. I hid behind the pantry door and practiced saying *some* of them. There was the one unspeakable word: six letters long, beginning with the fourteenth letter of the alphabet. I never practiced saying that one.

But I did want to talk about slavery. I wanted to know about it and hear about it. I wanted to know why.

I suppose I am tampering with *IT* now by writing about *IT*, talking about *IT*, *out loud*. What draws me in is wondering and imagining how one particular event impacted an individual or a family. I have wondered about this for a long time; What did it feel like to *finally* be free?

HISTORICAL BACKGROUND NOTES

On December 20, 1860, South Carolina became the first state to secede from the Union. By late February, Alabama, Florida, Georgia, Louisiana, Mississippi, and Texas would follow.

Most Southerners believed they had every right to break away from the Union as was stated in the Declaration of Independence: "It is the right of the people to alter or abolish" a government that denies the rights of its citizens. They believed Lincoln would deny their rights to own slaves.

When Abraham Lincoln took the oath of office on March 4, 1861, it was a dangerous situation for the new president. He stated a warning in his inaugural address: "No state . . . can lawfully get out of the Union." And he pledged that there would be no war unless the South started it.

On April 12, 1861, the Southern Confederacy bombarded Fort Sumter off the South Carolina coast. This act of aggression is what started the Civil War.

The state of Virginia had not yet ratified their vote to secede. That would come on May 23, 1861.

With the bombing of Fort Sumter, three field hands— Shepard Mallory, Frank Baker, and James Townsend— belonging to Colonel Mallory of Virginia had been instructed to build artillery batteries along the coastline for the Confederacy.

Later, the three learned of the colonel's plan to send them farther south, where they would be separated from their families and put to work constructing other artillery batteries for the rebels.

On the very evening Virginians were celebrating their secession vote, the three men had been instructed to build an artillery battery near Fort Monroe, one of the only Union-controlled outposts in the South. That very night the three men made a courageous decision and a pact. They would not do as they were instructed. In fact, they decided they would not build another.

Risking a beating or far worse, rather than follow Colonel Mallory's command, the men took a boat across the James River and gave themselves over to the Union at Fort Monroe.

Days later Colonel Mallory sent a messenger requesting the return of his property as he was entitled to do under the law. The 1850 Fugitive Slave Act required citizens to assist in the recovery of fugitive slaves and runaways.

Under the law the men should have been returned to Colonel Mallory.

The general of Fort Monroe, Benjamin F. Butler, flatly refused the request, citing that since Virginia was now a "foreign country" having just days before seceded, he had no constitutional obligation to return the runaways. Instead, he would seize the three men as "contraband of war," property to be used by the enemy against the Union.

As word spread that these men were now granted a

place of safety and protection under the contraband of war ruling, other enslaved people began flocking to "Freedom's Fortress."

The fort quickly became overcrowded, as they were not equipped to handle the growing number of people arriving daily looking for refuge. Eventually, makeshift villages were established to accommodate the displaced people.

Some of the people felt the conditions were far worse than what they left at the plantations they fled from. Some were happy to experience a degree of liberty and autonomy, to begin to consider for themselves what independence meant personally to them. For some it was self-determination; they could decide for themselves how to spend their time. Or they could live with their families and acquire work in order to support them. Through all of these transitions, people wanted their children educated.

Schools were started and people sought education to better their lives. Some people looked upon the contraband of war policy as a way of creating a brand new self. Some people looked upon the migration of enslaved people to Freedom's Fortress as the beginning of the end of slavery as we knew it in the United States.

TIME LINE

ON SEPTEMBER 18, 1850, the Fugitive Slave Law was passed by the United States Congress as part of the compromise between the Southern slaveholding states and the Northern states. The law allowed slave hunters to seize alleged fugitive slaves without due process of law, and prohibited anyone from aiding escaped fugitives or obstructing their recovery.

ON NOVEMBER 6, 1860, Abraham Lincoln was elected the sixteenth president of the United States (the first Republican), defeating opponents Stephen A. Douglas, John C. Breckinridge of the Southern Democrats, and John Bell of the new Constitutional Union Party.

ON DECEMBER 20, 1860, in response to Abraham Lincoln's election as president of the United States, a special session of the South Carolina legislature convened and voted unanimously to secede from the Union.

ON JANUARY 3, 1861, the Delaware state legislature officially and overwhelmingly rejected a proposal to leave the Union and join the Confederacy. There was little expectation that Delaware would vote to secede; of the twenty thousand blacks who lived there, only eighteen hundred were enslaved.

ON JANUARY 9, 1861, the *Star of the West*, an unarmed merchant steamer chartered by the War Department to transport troops and supplies from New York City to Fort Sumter, in Charleston Harbor, South Carolina, was fired upon and driven off by South Carolina.

ON JANUARY 9, 1861, the state of Mississippi became the second state to leave the Union.

ON JANUARY 10, 1861, Florida voted to secede.

ON JANUARY 11, 1861, Alabama voted to secede from the Union.

ON JANUARY 18, 1861, in reaction to the secession of the Southern states, Massachusetts offered President Lincoln "such aid in men and money as he may request, to maintain the authority of the general Government."

ON JANUARY 19, 1861, Georgia became the fifth state to secede from the Union.

ON JANUARY 26, 1861, the Louisiana legislature voted to withdraw from the Union.

ON JANUARY 29, 1861, the state of Kansas entered the Union as a free state, its constitution prohibiting slavery.

ON FEBRUARY 1, 1861, Montgomery, Alabama, was chosen capital of the Confederate States of America. The capital would move to Richmond on May 20 after Virginia joined the Confederacy.

ON FEBRUARY 1, 1861, Texas seceded.

ON FEBRUARY 11, 1861, President-elect Abraham Lincoln began his twelve-day journey to Washington, DC, to assume the presidency. It was from the Great Western Railroad depot in Springfield, Illinois, that he gave one of his most touching speeches.

ON FEBRUARY 18, 1861, Jefferson Davis was appointed the First Provisional President of the Confederate States of America.

On MARCH 4, 1861, Abraham Lincoln was inaugurated as the sixteenth president of the United States. In his address he spoke to rebellious Southerners: "In your hands, my dissatisfied fellow-countrymen, and not in mine, is the momentous issue of civil war. The Government will not assail you. You can have no conflict without being yourselves the aggressors."

ON MARCH 21, 1861, Confederate leaders were eager to emphasize the irreconcilable differences between North and South. Vice President Alexander Stephens delivered an impassioned speech stating: "Our new Government is founded upon . . . the great truth, that the Negro is not equal to the white man; that slavery—subordination to the superior race—is his natural and moral condition."

ON APRIL 12-13, 1861, Fort Sumter in Charleston Harbor, South Carolina, was attacked by artillery. After exchanging fire

for thirty-four hours, the fort surrendered. The bombardment of Fort Sumter marked the beginning of the American Civil War.

ON APRIL 15, 1861, President Lincoln issued a proclamation of war and a call for volunteers to suppress the rebellion.

ON APRIL 17, 1861, Virginia secedes.

ON APRIL 19, 1861, the Sixth Massachusetts Regiment was attacked by a mob of pro-Southern advocates while marching through Baltimore.

ON APRIL 29, 1861, Maryland rejected secession.

ON MAY 6, 1861, Arkansas seceded from the Union.

ON MAY 16, 1861, the Kentucky General Assembly enacted a declaration of neutrality.

ON MAY 23, 1861, in the evening as Confederate sympathizers celebrated Virginia's decision to secede, three male slaves—Frank Baker, James Townsend, and Shep Mallory—rowed a small boat across the James River to Fort Monroe, one of the only Union-controlled outposts in the South, surrendering themselves for having given aid to the rebels.

ON MAY 24, 1861, General Butler refused to return the runaways, declaring them "contraband of war." As Virginia was now

a foreign country, he had no obligation to return the men. Word spread rapidly and within days, dozens, and then hundreds, more runaways appeared at the gates seeking safety.

ON MAY 29, 1861, Richmond, Virginia became the Confederate capital.

ON JUNE 8, 1861, Tennessee voted to secede.

ON JUNE 18, 1861, President Lincoln signed legislation authorizing the United States Sanitary Commission, the relief agency created to provide care for the sick and wounded of the war.

ON JULY 17, 1861, the United States government started issuing paper money.

ON AUGUST 6, 1861, Lincoln signed the First Confiscation Act. Congress authorized Union forces to confiscate slaves used against the government, legitimizing General Benjamin Butler's policy of designating runaway slaves as contraband of war.

ON AUGUST 7, 1861, Confederate soldiers set fire to the city of Hampton, Virginia, burning it to the ground so that it would not fall into the hands of the enemy.

ON SEPTEMBER 3, 1861, Reverend Lewis C. Lockwood of the American Missionary Association became the first missionary to the freedmen at Fort Monroe. He made arrangements for weekday and Sabbath meetings, and organized weekday and evening schools.

ON SEPTEMBER 17, 1861, Mary S. Peake held her first class at Fort Monroe.

ON DECEMBER 1, 1861, a bill was introduced in Congress to end slavery in the District of Columbia.

ON DECEMBER 10, 1861, Kentucky was accepted as the thirteenth Confederate State.

ON FEBRUARY 22, 1862, Mary S. Peake died of tuberculosis. Her tombstone reads: *The First Teacher of the Freedmen at Fortress Monroe, VA.*

ON MARCH 13, 1862, Congress prohibited the return of fugitive slaves.

ON APRIL 10, 1862, President Lincoln requested that Congress pass a resolution to offer any slave state compensation from the federal government in return for enacting a bill of gradual emancipation.

ON APRIL 16, 1862, President Lincoln signed into law the District of Columbia Compensated Emancipation Act. It freed all slaves within the capital and paid every slaveholder three hundred dollars for each slave.

ON MAY 20, 1862, the Homestead Act of 1862 was signed by President Lincoln.

ON JUNE 19, 1862, Congress outlawed slavery in all territories belonging to the United States of America.

ON JULY 17, 1862, Congress passed the Militia Act of 1862, declaring that African-Americans could be utilized by the United States Army and Navy.

ON JULY 17, 1862, Congress passed the Second Confiscation Act, decreeing that any Confederate official whose land was occupied by the Union who did not surrender within sixty days would have his slaves freed.

ON SEPTEMBER 22, 1862, President Lincoln issued the preliminary Emancipation Proclamation, declaring all slaves in active rebellion states would be freed if said states didn't end their fighting and rejoin the Union by January 1, 1863.

ON JANUARY 1, 1863, President Lincoln signed the executive order known as the Emancipation Proclamation. He would later call it "the great event of the nineteenth century."

calico
girl

Prologue

     ∾

All is well now for Callie. But things did not start out that way. The days that led to these were many and hard. There were times when she supposed life could be nothing else. Looking back, it was only the world as she knew it. But the world is vast. Time brings many changes.

In time war came and changed her world. It started April of 1861—the opening of the Civil War. Callie could not have known what was to come, but her world was ending.

Out of the old, something new was beginning. She became what she is today because of that.

Many stories come out of long ago and hard times. It was not so long ago. But the times were hard indeed. This is Callie Wilcomb's story.

PART ONE

The World
As Callie Knew It

On April 12, 1861, the Southern Confederacy bombarded Fort Sumter off the South Carolina coast. This act of violence is what started the war between the North and the South: the Civil War. The North was industrialized. There were factories. Most of the wealth in the South was held in land and slaves and their labor. Southerners had to raise money quickly. Many plantation owners were forced to sell their slaves and livestock to pay off their debts in support of the war effort.

CHAPTER ONE

Callie

April 22, 1861

Sunlight poured into Suse's bedroom, making Callie feel even more weighed down with what the day was bringing. Callie wished she could have stopped the new day from rising. Morning was her favorite time of the day, but not this morning. The world was spinning and churning out of control around her.

The hurt inside her was deep as a well; she felt she was drowning. She wished she could open herself up to release what made her feel so numb and silent.

The crying and wailing of Callie's stepmother, Mama Ruth, could be heard all the way to Mister Henry's house from the Quarters. He had forbidden her to leave the cabin. Callie's papa, Hampton, was with her and Little Charlie, who was only two years of age. Callie prayed her little brother was too young to truly know or remember what was happening this horrible day.

Mister Henry was selling the last of his able-bodied slaves to Mister Arnold Tweet, a Mississippi cotton farmer. This included Albert and John, and Callie's stepbrother Joseph. He was fifteen and could handle a plow. Joseph may not have been a seasoned slave but he could do a man's day. He was considered a man.

Yesterday, when Mister Henry announced his intentions to sell his slaves in order to raise money for the war that was coming, Mistress Catherine was nowhere to be found. Papa found no fault with her, though.

"Callie," he said, taking his daughter's hands into his. Papa only did this when he wanted her to understand the thing that was so impossible for her to understand: the intricate and peculiar family ties that bound master and slave together.

Mistress Catherine was wholly white. She was Papa's half sister. They shared the same father but not the same mother. Hampton's mother was a slave. The child had to follow the condition of the mother. Hampton never got to know and love his mother. She was taken away from him and sold shortly after he was born. And so, he was brought up right alongside his half sisters, Catherine and Eloise.

"We must not blame Mistress Catherine for being such a timid soul," Papa explained, trying to soothe Callie. "Matters such as these were never in her spirit to conduct." But Callie could not even look at her papa. He gently turned her face to his.

Then Papa reminded her, "Callie, you must remember, we have a kind mistress in Catherine. It is because of her that you and I are better off than so many other folk." Callie knew he meant, better off than even Mama Ruth, Joseph, and Little Charlie, too. And this knowledge hurt her even more.

"We must abide as best as we can until there are better times," he told her.

"For now, Callie, in your mistress, Catherine, we have *some* protection," he explained, still holding her hand. "Try to understand."

Callie could not keep her gaze on her papa's face. He wanted her to look into his eyes so she would understand his heart. But Callie could not control the tears that filled her eyes and spilled down her face. Callie knew all too well what he meant but she had promised herself to refuse to try to understand. Papa brought her in close while she cried.

"I don't know how I can live in this world without Joseph," she whispered to Papa through her tears. And I don't know how he is supposed to live in the world alone without us, his family."

Papa tried explaining to her the way things worked in

the world they lived in. But Callie could not make right sense of the things he told her. She often wondered how her mistress, Catherine, could have a brother in her papa, who was born a slave, and was promised to never be sold away, and when he became a certain age he was given his freedom. This promise was kept. It would happen for Callie because she was Hampton's daughter. How could it be, she wondered, that Mister Henry could have the say in pulling Papa's family apart?

Once, long ago, Callie asked her papa how he felt when he became free. He looked at her and smiled.

"It was wonderful and strange," he said. "I felt like myself, only bigger inside. There was something that made me feel as if I was newly born. When your time comes, the star that shines for you will shine even brighter, my Callista," he said, hugging her to his chest.

Her papa promised her when she received her freedom papers he would take some of the money he was saving to send her to school in the North.

"You have a questioning mind, Callie. You have opinions about everything. You want to know about the world around you. Your heart is strong and you need this strength to live in this kind of world," he said. "Learn everything you can, so that you can bring that wisdom to others. You will make a good teacher."

And yet, when Callie thought on these things she wondered how freedom would truly feel for her.

How will I be able to go to school in the North and leave those I love when they do not have their freedom? This freedom can never be true for Mama Ruth, Joseph, and Little Charlie. Mister Henry owns them outright. He has never made—nor will he ever make—such a promise to them. He has said so many times, and this day proves it.

Most every night before she went to sleep, Callie thought about slave property and ownership.

I wonder on wonders why the world has been made this way. If God made this world why is this not a good world for the slave? It doesn't seem good to me.

My mother died before I could know her. At my birth, Papa says, something went wrong as she brought me into the world. But when Mister Henry finally allowed Mistress to send for the doctor, it was too late.

Sometimes in the secret of the night when things were quiet and still, Callie would let herself feel such hateful thoughts about Mister Henry.

"He robbed me of my mother," she would cry. Then her anguish would turn toward Suse.

But when these times happened, rivers of sadness would pour over Callie because she knew her feelings were not right. It was not Suse's fault, Callie knew, even though she took after Mister Henry too much for her liking.

Then Callie would think how this would hurt Mama Ruth.

I have a good mother in Mama Ruth, she would tell herself. *She knew my mother, and sometimes tells me about her. Stories are all anyone can give to me. And I know I have to be satisfied with that until I can make my own.*

If this is the world God has made, I wish God had made another. I do not like this one. It is not good, so why is it called the Good Book?

These thoughts were in Callie's mind and her heart and she did not know how she would forget them. Daily she prayed that God would welcome her to heaven, even with her bad thoughts. *I do not want to go to the other place for all the lost souls.*

"I do not want to understand," she finally told her papa as she had told herself so many times when she was alone in the night and no one was listening.

"This is no way to live. These laws are hateful and awful, and have such ugliness about them. We are a family. You, Mama Ruth, Joseph, Little Charlie, and I are a family," she repeated. "It is wrong to break apart a family—to include some and leave out others."

The night before the sale, Mister Henry ordered Callie to stay in the room of his daughter, Suse, until his business was complete the next morning. Suse was Callie's responsibility. Besides helping in the kitchen and some housework, Callie had to tend to Suse. When Suse had need of her or when she was sick, Callie slept on a pallet on the floor next to Suse's bed. But this night, Callie hardly slept.

The news had caused such a commotion, such a mess after Mister Henry announced his intentions. All day long Mister Henry's announcement rang in Callie's ears like an out-of-tune bell. And all day long she had plotted and planned what she would do when night fell and the house was settled and quiet.

The mess and commotion would only grow worse come the next morning when Mister Arnold Tweet arrived to collect his property.

Suse had fallen asleep hours ago. But Callie's mind twisted and turned. Her heart pounded and ached. She lay on her floor bedding, fully dressed, waiting for the moment when there was no movement from the floorboards, letting her know that everyone in the Big House was asleep. The house was quiet.

Callie had already made up her mind.

She sprang from the floor. Even without a lit candle to guide her, she knew where to go. Walking through the darkness, Callie knew where to place her steps so that she missed the floorboards and the stairs that creaked. She knew how to push in on the door handle when she opened the door to Suse's room so there was no noise. Callie had become practiced at this. Many times before this she had sneaked out of the Big House. Sometimes she would be with Suse, maybe to count the stars or wish on them. Sometimes Callie would go alone. And when she was alone she would speak her wish for freedom out loud to the night. Or she'd steal away to her cabin where her family slept, and she would sit and listen to the quietness and their breathing.

She hated those nights when it was demanded that she sleep in Suse's room.

This time Callie was not counting stars or seeking the comfort of her family. Callie's heart raced. She moved quickly through the night heading to the kitchen house, careful not to disturb Elsa, the cook, who slept there. Callie grabbed the bundle of food and supplies she had hidden in the kitchen earlier that day. She hoped there was enough for two. If not, Papa had taught them how to catch fish with their bare hands. Joseph was even better at fishing this way than Papa.

She headed to the old barn. Joseph was housed there with the two other men. The barn was not of much use anymore. Mister Henry had already sold most of the farm animals. What was left of them could all be kept in the smaller barn.

Callie had decided there was nothing left to do but for the two of them to run away together. She had heard stories of slaves who had escaped their masters, but she had never heard the outcome of their fate. Her only hope was that by sunup they would have gotten far enough away from Belle Hill Farm. Callie would not allow herself to think of all that she loved that she was leaving behind.

When things were settled, they would somehow get

word to Papa and Mama Ruth to let them know they were safe and free.

There was only a sliver of a moon. Callie went to the side of the barn where the boards were slack. She wiggled the boards to loosen the nails until she had enough room to squeeze through.

It was dark and musty. The air was still and close. She could see no shapes, but she could hear someone whimper.

"Joseph," Callie called. "It's me, Callie," she whispered across the darkness.

"Callie-girl? What are you doing here?"

"I've come to set you free, Joseph. I can't let him do this to you. I can't let you be sold away from us. We can run away together."

"Oh, Callie-girl," Joseph said, trying to keep his sobs quiet. She could hear the chains rattling as he turned in her direction.

"Papa already tried, Callie. He came and talked to all of us earlier tonight," Joseph admitted.

"Did Mama Ru . . . ?"

"No, Papa said she wanted to come but I asked him to keep her away from here."

"Joseph, what are we going to do?"

"Unless you brought something that can break these chains, I'm going nowhere until morning."

"Oh, Joseph," she cried. And when she reached out

to hug him she could feel that his face was wet from tears.

"Oh, Joseph, what can we do?" Callie sobbed. "What can we do?"

"You remember what Papa told us about our stars?" Callie nodded her head. "I'll remember them, Callie-girl. Will you?"

"Yes, Joseph. I promise I will. I promise."

CHAPTER TWO

Callie and Suse

That same day

S use sat on the bench of her mirrored dressing table.
She was brushing her hair and humming a song a
little too loudly.

"Ouch," she shouted while the brush fell to the floor.
She wanted Callie to notice her or speak to her, say something to her. But Callie's attention was someplace else.
She never even looked in Suse's direction. She lay on the
floor facing the opposite wall.

When Suse realized Callie was paying her no mind,

she put the brush down a little too hard on the table. Then she got the high back chair from the other side of her room and placed it against the wall that was farthest from the window.

"Now, Callie Wilcomb, you listen to me. You get up from this floor. You must sit up and keep to this chair," Suse said, pointing quickly and with authority. Callie was slow to move, but Suse could not sit still. Every other minute or two she would get up from her dressing table and sashay around the room, moving past the window for a peek of what was going on in the yard as she continued humming her song and brushing her hair.

Callie was flooded with memories and sad thoughts.

"Today," Suse announced, hesitantly turning toward Callie, "you may not brush my hair this morning. I will do that for myself!"

Callie did not care the least bit about the knots in Suse's hair. She did not want to notice the girl, but Suse demanded her attention. She wondered if this might be Suse's way of caring for her. Suse was so hard to understand.

Suse knew Callie balked at brushing out the tangles of her hair more than she did. Still, it was too much effort to consider the twisting and turnings of Suse's mind. Callie sat sideways on the chair, her head turned away from Suse and the window, and leaned against the back of the chair. She was limp as wet clothes hanging on the clothesline.

From the bedroom window you could see the whole

of the farmyard. Suse was delighted to watch what was happening. She had never seen the likes of a slave sale before. Normally, Mister Henry kept these matters private, preferring to go into town to the slave market alone or with one of the overseers. But the news of the war turned everything upside down. Out of convenience to Mister Tweet and an eagerness to get this sale over with, Mister Henry conducted his business right in the farmyard!

Suse could not contain her excitement. She wanted to chatter about what was going on in the farmyard. Callie was the only one nearby.

Callie had made it clear she did not want to know one little thing of the misery Mister Henry Warren was making this day.

"Albert and John are already strapped into the wagon for the long trip south," she exclaimed with excitement in her voice. "Now Mister Tweet is looking Joseph over."

It was of little consequence to Callie that Suse announced every interaction. Callie already knew what was happening because Mama Ruth's cries grew even louder.

Finally, Suse slapped Callie's arm with the back of her hairbrush so that she would look up when she spoke to her.

"Callie, now, you pay attention to me," Suse demanded.

Callie looked at Suse as if for a moment she did not remember who she was.

"It hurts me to hear my Mama Ruth cry," she told her. "I should be with her. I think she needs me now."

"Just you never mind about that, Callie. I need you more. Daddy and I insist you are here in my room with me!

"This is for your own good—*our* own good! You know Daddy knows what is best for us all. He has his family and all these other mouths to feed. So don't you go and bring temper to me, Callie! I just won't have it." She turned away from Callie but kept right on talking.

"There is great need for farm labor in the Deep South," Suse explained, sounding so much like Mister Henry.

"The war has started, Callie. You know this!" Suse added, raising her voice almost to a scream as she went to her dressing table and took something from the drawer.

"Just look at this and see for yourself." She held up a newspaper advertisement so that Callie could see it. She read the advertisement, pointing out every word:

Wanted, Slave Labor!
In the South, Cotton is King.
There is Cash Money to be made!
Each slave is sold for $2000.

Callie only nodded. She refused to look at Suse or the paper she was holding. It was not temper that kept her from looking. Callie was feeling lost, as lost and disoriented as she did that night when the two girls went exploring in Old Man Calper's Cave. That was the night Callie saw a side of Suse she had not seen before. That night Suse ran away and left Callie behind alone in Calper's Cave.

The fear overtook her, growing through her body like weeds. She didn't think she would ever stop shaking. Her fright was so strong and the cave was so dark, she felt that she had all but disappeared and ended up in the awful place for all the lost souls.

After Papa and Joseph rescued her, and brought her home, they all three sat together on the step of their cabin. Callie would not let go of Papa's hand.

"I thought I was going to be lost forever," Callie whispered to Papa.

"Oh, Callie-girl. You can never be lost from me!" Papa exclaimed.

"But I was. I didn't think I would see you or Joseph, or Mama Ruth, or Little Charlie . . . again," she cried.

"Pshaw," Papa laughed dismissively, and hugged her. Then Papa looked up toward the heavens, moving his head from side to side this way and that as if he were searching for something important he left behind up there. Papa's actions made Callie laugh in spite of herself, which made Joseph laugh too.

"Look up, Callie. You too, Joseph," Papa said, pointing upward. "Can you find the Big Dipper?" he asked.

"There it is!" Joseph pointed triumphantly.

"Now, listen to me, both of you. And I don't want you to *ever* forget what I am saying to you tonight." Joseph and Callie shook their heads and Papa spoke again.

"Wherever you are, wherever you go, or whatever

happens to you in this life, know that you can *never* be lost from me.

"If *ever* you find yourself thinking this way, stop it! You find those stars in the sky. Know that if you see those stars, the same stars that your mama and papa see, know you can never be lost from us. Those are your stars, Callista," he said. "Your name comes from those stars."

Callie blinked a few times and sniffled.

"And wherever we go, we never go alone. Family comes with us all the time, in our hearts, in our minds."

Callie repeated the thing Papa had told her before.

"Yes, that's right." Papa said, laughing. "Once you belong to a family, you are never alone. You always belong to them."

"Those stars sure shine pretty tonight," Joseph said, smiling and taking in a big breath of the night air.

"Because you are mine, you will always be safe," Papa said, and put his arms around both his children, wrapping them up in a safe cocoon. Callie let herself feel how good it was to hear Papa's breathing and the beating of his heart.

"I am safe," Callie told Papa. "Because you are mine, I am safe."

Suse and Callie loved to explore the world around them. It was at these times when the two could be free to be themselves and the roles they had to play in life would drop away. They could act as friends. They could be brave together. They would run and yell and giggle. They would dream and imagine and make wishes on stars or skip rocks on the fishing pond.

They had explored as far as they dared go in the forests around Belle Hill Farm. They had explored all of the attic rooms of the house. It was the times like these that every so often Callie forgot the rules between slave and master and she thought Suse did, too. Callie tried hard to remember these times when Suse was having one of her mean spells.

"I think I know that Suse likes me," Callie told Mama Ruth one day when the two were pulling weeds in the garden.

"I don't know what would make you think that," Mama Ruth said as she looked at Callie.

"She has said as much, in her way," Callie told Mama Ruth as she remembered the day when Suse explained to her the way things were between them and why they had to be that way.

"I could be closer to you, Callie—a lot closer to you," Suse had begun. "But there is a line Daddy says I must never ever cross."

"A line?" Callie had asked her. "What does that mean?"

"A line between you and me—a line between us and all of you," she had gestured, trying to make Callie understand.

That afternoon the two girls were outside in the tobacco fields. This was before the soil had grown barren, but Suse kicked the tobacco plant with her boots, as if she did not care one whit for the hands that would pick it come harvest time.

"Yes, a line, he said. I asked him how come, and do you know what he said?" she had asked, very proud that she had an answer Callie did not.

"What did he say?"

"'It is simple. This is our way of life,' he told me." Suse hesitated. "But sometimes, Callie, I *want* to be friends. I *feel* like I want to, truly I do. I want to cross the line right now and be close to you like I am with Jenny or Rose Mallory. But I cannot. A good daughter does what her daddy asks of her," she had explained.

"What about your mother, Mistress Catherine? What does he say about Papa and her being family relations? What does he say about that?" Callie had asked.

"Daddy says that is of no concern and means nothing. Her father, Grandfather Edward, was an Englishman. That means he was misguided against our ways, and taught Mother to be the same."

Callie never forgot that day in the field. She never talked about it to Suse again. The talk of a line that would never allow Callie to be close to Suse felt bad and it caused something deep inside of her to hurt.

It is a strange thing—it rips us all apart—slave and master.

Now that same something inside of Callie was hurting. And it felt worse than being lost in that dark cave or walking through the tobacco fields ever could.

"Come and stand next to me in the mirror," Suse said.

It was clear Callie especially did not want to play this game. Suse went over to the chair where Callie was sitting and dragged her to her feet.

"I am sure to be taller than you now, Callie. I'm wearing my new boots with the heels." But Suse was not any taller. Callie was still a half head taller than her even though she wore her flat-heeled work boots.

The two girls stood in the mirror looking at each other's reflection. They couldn't be more different. They were an odd pair looking mix-matched and out of place. Suse was wearing her red plaid taffeta dress, which was shiny and smooth. It made a *swishy swishy* noise as she walked.

In contrast, Callie wore the colorless rough-cut cloth of linen and wool. It was a heavy, coarse, and scratchy material, a shapeless dress that hung off her shoulders like a sack. Mama Ruth called it osnaburg cloth or linsey-woolsey cloth. Some called it slave cloth. Mister Henry insisted she wear it. It marked her as a slave.

With an underslip it could be warm to wear in the winter. Either way, the dress was too hot to wear in the summer months. Callie hated the clothes she had to wear. Standing next to Suse in her fine clothes made Callie hate the dress even more—not because of the finery of Suse's clothes; it was not something she would choose for herself to wear either. But she had no choice.

If she could choose anything to wear, Callie would not choose silk or velvet or brocade or taffeta as Suse did. Callie would choose calico. It was a simple cotton cloth.

Callie loved those times when Mama Ruth would tell her of when she and Hampton were first married and Mama Ruth and Joseph moved into their cabin.

"You were still as much as a baby," Mama Ruth once began. "I had a little boy, but I never had a little girl." She smiled.

"You were the sweetest and happiest-looking thing. I swaddled you in the softest thing I could find. It was calico. I patched together some few pieces from my scraps basket that I keep until I had a little blanket for you. You loved that blanket.

"When you grew out of the need of a blanket, you wouldn't let it go. So, I made a dress out of it. You were too little to do any farmwork, and I would not put you in that slave cloth," she said, laughing, and Callie laughed too.

"You seemed to like the look and feel of it so much," Mama Ruth added. "You'd point to the little dainty flower pattern on the dress. 'Pretty flower,' you'd say.

"So, I called you Callie, my Calico Girl. I saved that little dress for as long as I could. If I could, I'd dress you in calico right now."

Calico cloth was not for a party dress or a Sunday-go-to-meeting kind of thing like velvet, or silk, or taffeta. It was just a sweet, plain, smooth cloth, not fancy at all. It could have an all-over flower pattern or stripes or little designs in the cloth.

Callie once tried explaining to Suse what she would rather wear if she had a choice in the matter: "It is just a plain cloth, but, it is the cloth I like the best." But Suse was not interested in hearing what she had to say.

Just then, Callie heard a noise. It was Suse. She had gone into her clothes closet where she had all kinds of dresses. Callie heard her rustling around, like she was digging for treasure and mumbling to herself.

"Now, where is it?" Suse loved to talk, even if it was to no one at all. "Where is that old thing," she kept asking herself. "It should have been right . . .

"Here it is, Callie! Finally, I found what I was looking for!" Suse announced.

"This is for you," Suse said, thrusting her green taffeta and velvet party dress into Callie's hand.

"Don't ever say I never did anything nice for you! I'm giving you my *party* dress. Even though I have outgrown it, now at least you have something pretty and shiny to look at during these hard times. Maybe your mama Ruth can fix it for you. Mother says your mama Ruth is the best seamstress for hundreds of miles around."

Callie held the dress in her hands like a rag and still said nothing. But that did not stop Suse from chattering. So she went back to the chair and sat down while Suse rattled on.

"Daddy says with this great war coming we all must do our part to help the effort to defend our way of life here, Callie. Once Daddy settles his business affairs here at home, he is leaving us. Do you understand? He is leaving us to go to fight in the war!

"That's a sacrifice, too, Callie! That's a *big* sacrifice," Suse said beginning to choke up and cry. "Everybody has to do something, Callie—you and me and Joseph and your stepmother, Mama Ruth!"

Now Callie felt it was Suse who had crossed a line.

Callie thought about Mama Ruth right then. She thought about what Mama Ruth had said about forgiving others. Callie wondered if Mister Henry's selling Joseph to pay his debts was something she could forgive. Callie would not mind one little bit if this was something she could not do. Callie knew she could not forgive him. And she had decided that she would not, not ever.

"I'm tired, Callie," Suse said, finally having worn her own self out. She went to her bed and lay there. Callie rose from the chair and walked to the window. She could hear the wagon as it went off down the road. She wanted to run to try to catch up to it to see Joseph one last time, but she knew Joseph was gone. Mister Henry was standing in the middle of the yard now, counting his money.

For a moment, he looked up at the window to see her standing there. A wide grin slid across his face.

"I'm going to see my Mama Ruth now," Callie told Suse. She walked out of her room before she could say anything to her about what she could or could not do. Callie walked right past Mister Henry and went to Mama Ruth in their cabin.

April, 1861, the war officially began. Everything rested on the energy and vigor of each blow the opposing sides could strike. At the start some felt the Union had two months to crush the Confederacy's morale.

The Union felt that an example had to be made of Virginia. If Virginia fell, it would strike terror into every other Southern state. Virginia was seen as unprepared and could not get ready quickly enough for an immediate contest. Time was of the essence. Things had to move, and fast.

CHAPTER THREE

Henry Warren

May 17, 1861

As the sun rose on that morning, the master of the Belle Hill Plantation, Henry Warren, prepared to leave for the battlefield. He did not know what to expect, nor did he know how long the war would last. He only knew he had been given the summons, and he had to heed the call. He was neither a soldier nor a farmer. He had been trained in the law. But Henry knew he had to do his part.

The Southern Confederacy had acted swiftly in the

bombardment of Fort Sumter in Charleston Harbor, South Carolina, the month before. The war had started. Henry's state of Virginia had not yet ratified their vote. South Carolina and six other southern states had now cast their lot with the Confederacy.

It was not a question of *if* he would return, for he knew he would, but in what shape, what condition, what circumstances? It was a risk, but one he was willing to take.

Every Southerner had a stake in this war. Those who agreed with this noble cause had to take a stand to defend their way of life. It was a matter of individual pride and state's honor. What more could they do?

Henry Warren had taken care of his affairs. He sold what property he could. He paid his debts. This was help for the South. Each and every man, woman, and child had to do his share.

Life had moved so quickly.

Henry told his manservant, William, to do a final check of the supply wagon. Necessities and provisions were few. Henry would have to bring as many supplies as he could carry with him. William would be accompanying him, to attend to his master's daily needs.

It angered Henry mightily that he wanted Hampton at his side. Freedman or not, Henry wanted Hampton Wilcomb to accompany him. He was not above using the force of law. But his wife would not hear of it.

Catherine would not go back on her word to him. It had been stated and agreed to in Henry and Catherine's marriage papers that the freedman Hampton Wilcomb, her father's son; his wife, Sara; and heirs and children of that union belonged in the Wilcomb family. No other person could manage, direct, or have any say over them without express permission or consent from the Wilcombs, and now that meant Catherine, the only surviving member of the family.

Even after Henry's strong appeal, at a most important hour such as this, Catherine refused to surrender her control and consent.

"We have discussed this matter. I would rather not have it brought up to me again," Catherine said, dismissing the conversation. "Let people say what they will; this is a matter of *my* family pride and honor. I cannot go back on my word to my brother." Though Henry had pressed the matter again, the mistress of the plantation was resolute. It angered him even more when so very much was at stake.

To settle the matter once and for all, Catherine appealed to Henry's sense of honor and protective nature.

"Don't you agree we will need just as much help here?" Catherine began. "With most of the able-bodied slaves sold or sent South you cannot leave us here without help and completely defenseless. Hampton should stay here."

With that kind of argument Henry could pursue the matter no further. Looking back, Henry regretted that he had even allowed himself into such a marriage agreement with his wife's family.

The family had made their massive fortunes in textiles and indigo both here and abroad. Henry knew he and his heirs would gain much by the union, so he had agreed with the decision.

Besides, what was the life of one slave worth, considering the fortune he would one day inherit? The slave Hampton was raised side by side with the Wilcomb children, Catherine and her sister, Eloise. Edward Wilcomb had always wanted a son, and now he had one, and even gave the slave his last name. Catherine had felt as close to Hampton as she did her sister. He was the brother she never had, she said.

As a boy, the slave Hampton was quick, smart, and kind. He grew up to be hardworking and strong. He learned to be loyal, because he was treated as if he was one of the family. He felt bound by blood to love and protect the family he was born into. But that did not include his new master, who had married into the family.

Though Hampton was no longer a slave, Henry could never think of him as anything else. Hampton was a good wagon master. He was in charge of the horses; he was trusted with them, and with good reason. Hampton handled cash. He bought and sold products for the plantation and made the decision on the price. He was honest and forthright in his dealings and Catherine insisted he receive a salary, small as it were. He was everything Edward could have asked for in a son, everything Henry, a man of law, lacked.

"Fetch Hampton," Henry finally told William. At that moment, his wife and daughter stepped into the yard. Suse broke away from her mother's grasp and ran to put her arms around her father.

"Oh, Papa, Papa," Suse sobbed, running into her father's arms. Her tears splattered his uniform, leaving dark gray splotches. "Do you have to leave us?"

"Suse, my Suse, my dear, sweet daughter," he said, trying to comfort her.

Henry looked at Catherine, his eyes demanding she do something. But Catherine ignored her husband's concern. Instead of taking it up with Catherine, he kneeled to face his daughter. He took his daughter's face in his hands and kissed her forehead.

"Remember, my darling daughter, we all have to sacrifice and do our part for the cause. I promise I shall return to you in a few short months. Now, go on back to your mother," he said, which caused the girl to sob even more.

Then Henry, so overcome by his daughter's emotion, reached out and took both his wife and daughter into his arms. He finally felt the true gravity of what he was leaving behind.

"Should I never return," he said to them both, "if I fall, my last farewell is to you and my last remembrance is your expression of true love."

Catherine gently took her daughter by the shoulders and turned toward the house. The two were making their way back to the porch. Henry watched them. He hoped they would go inside and not watch him any further. It already was difficult enough to mount his horse and leave. But Suse and her mother stopped at the front porch.

As Henry Warren mounted Stock, the best horse left in his stable, he looked on at all he was leaving behind. It grieved him, but what choice did he have? He had to protect and keep what was his.

Hampton and his daughter, Callie, emerged from behind the kitchen building brushing wood chips out of their hair and off their clothes. Henry regarded the slave who called himself free. Hampton put his hand on his daughter's shoulder.

"You should run along back to the Quarters now," Hampton directed his daughter. "Tell your mother I will be there directly." Without hesitation Callie did what she was told and ran in the direction of their cabin.

Henry Warren watched Hampton.

Yes, he was a good, loyal, obedient worker, Henry thought. The man had gumption. He had get-up about him. He almost gave the appearance of any white man, standing straight, tall, unbending. His coloring only gave the impression of someone who had stayed in the sun too long.

Henry would never say it out loud, but he admired him. There were times Henry admitted this to himself when he would watch the man with the horses. He admired the man's wit. The man had a good deal of common sense. He was a valuable asset and was well regarded by all who still lived at Belle Hill.

Henry admired Hampton as much as he despised him. He disliked looking into his face, which without question bore such a striking family resemblance to his wife's. Hampton's mannerisms, eye color, strong nose, and jawline were all of the Wilcomb family. Henry remembered the pride in Edward Wilcomb's eyes when he would regard his son from afar, though he saved contempt and mistrust for his daughter's husband.

Hampton spoke too well. He had too many thoughts in his head. Henry hated him for the Wilcomb blood that ran through his veins; it made him more proud than any slave should have been in the face of his betters.

"Hampton," he shouted. "Come near to me!"

Hampton looked up and into the man's steel gray eyes. Henry Warren was not one to ever be in good humor, but Hampton knew how to address him. He was silent and attentive.

"In my absence," Henry began, "I charge you, to the last inch of your life, to take care of my family: your mistress, Catherine, my wife; and my daughter, Susanna; and *my* farm. I remind you of your *family* obligation to them.

"Through the years you have proven yourself to be honorable enough to be bound by this duty and responsibility. But if you are not honorable *enough* and you put your needs first . . . if you should run off, or any harm comes to my family, I promise you, Hampton, I shall find you. And when I find you, freedman or not, I *will* make you pay dearly for your transgression and your disobedience."

Henry Warren wanted everyone to hear and know this charge, though very few servants were left. It was a matter of honor. They would never favor him as they would Hampton, but they would know who was master of this house. He thought the look in Hampton's eyes told Henry he had done just that. But he was wrong. It was mostly just the opposite. Henry had no hold over Hampton, who was a freedman, and could not make demands or commands on his life.

It was a sad and empty departure. Not one Henry had ever hoped for, but he was willing to risk his life. In his heart, Henry did not know what the future would hold for them in these uncertain times.

As Henry Warren led his horse and wagon out onto the main road, it occurred to him that he had left something behind. The thought brushed through his mind for only a second. And then he realized that all the while he made pronouncements of his expectations to Hampton, he had said nothing. He neither agreed to nor disagreed with the commands Henry made to him.

Now Henry wondered if what he had said was compelling enough to cause Hampton to follow his orders and remain at Belle Hill. He wouldn't leave. Where would he go? Suddenly doubt filled Henry's mind.

But there was little Henry could do now, as the road took him farther and farther away, until Belle Hill was barely a speck on the horizon. He headed south toward the battlefield.

On April 17, 1861, the Virginia legislature adopted the Ordinance of Secession. On May 23 voters confirmed it, repealing Virginia's 1788 ratification of the Constitution of the United States. The North felt there was much to do before the rebellion would be crushed. It was said to be a desperate contest for superiority between men of the same race. Either the North or the South would become master of the continent.

CHAPTER FOUR

Hampton Wilcomb

May 23, 1861

In that next week, Hampton thought deeply about the charge Henry Warren had given him. He did not agree with it, nor did he say he would abide by his command. It was never his intention to stay behind. And even before the war had started he could go and come as he pleased. Catherine always knew Hampton wanted to join the fight, but he would need to do it in his own way, the way he felt was right.

He was a freedman, true enough, but still not permitted

to understand the magnitude of it—to think and act for himself, to freely choose, or to be and do as he saw fit for himself and his family. What Henry Warren had said did not take away the growing urge inside of him to leave and join the fight. Hampton would find some way to help defeat the rebels.

It was not the threat from Henry Warren that brought the worry to his mind and indecision to his feet that moonless night. It was the thought of leaving behind Ruth, Callie, and his little boy, Charlie—what was left of his family.

Hampton should not—he *could* not—leave without settling things with Ruth first. Only after would he speak with Catherine. After he was gone, Ruth would talk to the children. She was a good woman. He placed every trust in her.

Hampton paced up and down the road from his cabin, stopping just short of the entry gate. He wanted to pass on through and walk right out of the gate, onto the main road. Not even the overseer, John Sweeney, could stop him. But Sweeney, like many of the other white men, had gone off to fight in the war; few were left behind, none at Belle Hill Farm.

War had been declared. The new president had only been inaugurated a month before and was now fighting to regain half the country's territory. Hampton felt he wanted to do something, *anything*, that could help this new man, Lincoln, and the Union Army.

Hampton wanted to start walking and keep walking until he reached the James River. On the other side of the river was the Union Army outpost Fortress Monroe. He wasn't sure what he would do when he got there. He knew they would not allow him to fight, to enlist as a soldier, or handle a gun, as this was said to be a fight for superiority between men of the same race.

But where did that leave Hampton? At least he wanted to try. He had considered passing himself off as white. Others with his coloring had done the same, he knew. Never mind what would happen if he were discovered to be impersonating a soldier. Maybe it was a chance he would only take in such desperate times. But his heart was not completely made up in this direction. He never wanted to deny any part of himself. Though part of him was white, he was still a whole man, a whole person.

The soil on which the soldiers fought was his home. Hampton knew his talents and skills could be of use. He knew the people. He knew the waterways, trails, and the roads. He could give information about the enemy. He was a good horseman. He would be happy just to dig ditches with his bare hands, as long as it helped the Union Army defeat the rebellion.

Many, many years ago, the state of Virginia was known to be a leader in the struggle for this new country's independence. Hampton often wondered why secession was necessary.

He thought it was far too shortsighted of these many states to break away, to split off whenever new disagreements arose. Breaking apart would only make the nation weaker. Secession was no answer. Hampton's side had long been chosen. He felt secession was the coward's way, rather than facing the challenges that were laid down in the document that claimed this young country free and independent. He felt now perhaps there was too much independence.

As a boy, Hampton was quick and bright. He had been taught to read and think and figure, at the behest of his father, Edward Wilcomb. His studies began later than his sisters', but his eager mind and his father's devotion made learning a joyful task.

His education enabled him to read the document. Hampton knew what the words meant:

> *Prudence, indeed, will dictate that Governments*
> *long established should not be changed for light and*
> *transient causes . . .*

And from the many books and histories and philosophies he read came a roaring flame inside of him; he most wanted with all of his heart to see an end to that barbaric system of slavery. Hampton's father taught him so he knew and understood those words, as well:

> *We hold these truths to be self-evident,*
> *that all men are created equal,*
> *that they are endowed by their Creator*
> *with certain unalienable Rights,*
> *that among these are*
> *Life, Liberty, and the pursuit of Happiness.*

His father, Edward, was first and foremost a business-man who married late in life. When the children came, they came quickly—two daughters, Eloise, the elder, and then Catherine. With the birth of the second daughter, his wife, Mary Beth, became sick. All hopes of having a son were lost. But a son came to him though not of that union.

Still, Edward lavished love and attention onto all of his children: his two girls, but especially the son he always wanted. He taught the boy to reason and stand up for what he knew was right. But only in the confines of Belle Hill Farm.

Hampton could not be fully embraced by the Wilcomb family that Edward and Mary Beth created, because his mother, Elizabeth, was a slave. It was decided a year after Hampton's birth that Elizabeth be sent away, but not sold, and because of that Hampton had no memory of her. When he could speak, he would ask, "Where is my mother?" But he was never given an answer that suited him.

When Hampton turned ten, word came that his mother had been living in Baltimore and had died of pneumonia. He could not understand why he had not been allowed to know her. Why would his father, who claimed to love him as a son, refuse something that was allowed so many chil-dren in this world including his daughters: a mother. That left a loneliness in him that yielded to distrust for the man whom he loved and called Father.

Years later, Edward decided that Hampton would accompany him to England. It was Edward's thought to have the boy educated there. But Hampton would have nothing of it. He had fallen in love with Sara, the cook's daughter.

Hampton wanted to marry her and to travel to England together to start a new life, away from the shackles of this world they knew. Edward wanted the young man to expand his horizons for greater possibilities. There were times when Hampton would look back on his life and see that his father, in his own way, meant him well. Living with his family on Belle Hill Farm made him feel a sense of equality. But meeting Henry delivered such a shock and a reminder of what the world truly thought of him. Hampton knew the man never saw him as equal. In Henry's presence, it surprised Hampton he had to fight to be equal in his own home.

Hampton was tired of being considered as less. He had been treated as a slave all of his life, despite his freedom papers. He would have to carry them with him at all times, burning a hole in his breast pocket to his heart, the heart that yearned for freedom.

He wanted to be free of the bonds that pressed down on him and made him feel not as a man should feel, but as powerless as a child. He wanted freedom for himself and his family. He wanted true freedom for his people and this country! His country! His *home*!

Hampton's mind was made up. He *would* speak with Ruth tonight.

But all of that would have to wait for now. In the dim

moonlight, Hampton could see someone moving quickly toward the crossroad. Hampton hurried to pass through the gate. He ran to greet the traveler. It appeared to be Raleigh, James Townsend's boy from Colonel Stephen Mallory's plantation, the next farm over. Something was certainly not right about that.

CHAPTER FIVE

Raleigh Townsend

May 23, 1861
Later that same night

From a closer distance, Hampton was sure it was Raleigh.

He wondered what the boy was doing walking about alone at this hour of night, especially considering he was going in the opposite direction from his home. The Mallory farm was miles away and clear on the other side of a forest. The grove of wilderness separated the Mallory place from the Warren farm. It was the biggest and richest farm around; no one had more slaves than Colonel Mallory.

"Wooo hooo," Hampton called to the boy, and waved.

Hampton hoped no one was in need of medical care. With the war starting, doctors and their remedies were scarce to none now, outside of the army.

"Raleigh?" Hampton called, jogging to reach him, "is that you?" He could see that the boy had been running. Raleigh stopped and gave acknowledgment to Hampton. He put his hands on his knees, bending over to catch his breath.

"Yes . . . it's . . . me."

"Where you off to, Raleigh, and at this time of night?"

"Hampton . . ." the boy said, hardly able to talk and breathe at the same time. "Papa . . . sent me to . . ."

"Your papa? Is everything all right?" Hampton felt worried.

"Yes," he huffed, "he's fine. Well, I don't know. I pretty much think so."

"What happened?" Hampton felt alarmed. "When did you see him last?"

Hampton knew the boy's father, James Townsend, very well. James and two more of Mallory's field hands, Shep Mallory and Frank Baker, were being sent to build artillery placements for the Confederates. The three men were often gone for long periods of time. No slave wanted to fight on the side of the Confederacy and what they stood for, or help them in any way. Hampton felt himself lucky he was not forced to be in that position, to work for the rebels.

"Tonight," Raleigh began. "I mean just now." The boy could hardly get his words out straight, he was so overwhelmed. "Oh, Hampton. You won't believe what just happened. You just won't believe what we did. I can hardly believe it myself. But it's done, Hampton. It's done. It's done. And now it's started."

"Started what?" Hampton feared the worst. "Slow down and tell me. Make sense to me," Hampton said.

But Raleigh could hardly pause.

"Slow down now and catch your breath," Hampton told Raleigh as he placed a gentle hand on the boy's shoulder to calm him. After sitting quietly for a moment, Raleigh was finally beginning to breathe easier.

"Well," the boy began, "as always, Master Mallory sent Shep and Frank and Papa to build another artillery placement. This time he sent them just near to the Union Fortress Monroe at the James River. This time Papa brought me along with him—because of my iron-working skills, he said. But they didn't use them. I mean . . . they didn't do it. I mean . . . we didn't do it. I mean . . . we never built it."

Hampton's heart had been racing but now it was going even faster. As the breath left his lungs, he broke out into a cold sweat at Raleigh's words. He felt alarmed.

Hampton knew he had to be patient and hear the boy out. Raleigh was already having a hard enough time catching his breath. Hampton needed to know the why of the mystery that was unfolding.

"What happened? Speak plainly, Raleigh! Were you

caught? Did you escape? Did Colonel Mallory change his mind?"

"Not hardly," Raleigh began again. Hampton could see how shaken up the boy was.

"We did not build it, Hampton. . . . It had nothing to do with the colonel. Before we left, Papa and them got word that by the beginning of the week Master Mallory was planning to send the three of them farther down south, to South Carolina to do the same thing down there. Papa and Frank and Shep got to talking about it, for a *long* time, too. They all agreed, no matter what, they would not do it. They would find a way not to go. You know Papa doesn't believe in what they're doing."

"Yes," Hampton said encouragingly, eager for Raleigh to continue.

"So, instead of putting the artillery embankment at Fortress Monroe, we went across the river and turned ourselves over to the Union soldiers."

"You did what?!" Hampton's eyes grew wide. He could not believe what he was hearing out of the boy's mouth.

"Yes, we did." Raleigh took a moment to let his words settle over them. Hampton couldn't help but remark how much the boy looked like his father, as if he'd gained more than ten years just by telling this story.

"You see what I mean? Papa said it was bad enough Master Mallory forced them to work against the Yankees, but he said for sure he would not be sent into the Deep South, farther away from his family, to be of any more help to them. Papa said they didn't know what else they *could* do."

Hampton was stunned. His mind was racing. If Raleigh's story was true, Hampton could understand why the boy was so shaken up when he first arrived. Hampton himself needed time for this tale to catch up to his thinking mind.

"What happened? What did they do to you? The soldiers, I mean." Hampton wanted to know, fearing the worst. He had heard horrible tales of what the Northern army would do to slaves if they were caught, but thinking on it, it could be no worse than the capabilities of a slave's master.

A smile finally cracked on Raleigh's face, and Hampton felt some of the tension leave his body. "Nothing bad—nothing bad at all. They took us into the fort and kept us. They were friendly enough. They fed us, all we wanted to eat. Then they talked to us.

"At first, they asked us heaps and heaps of questions about why we came to the fort. We told them everything about what Colonel Mallory sent us to do . . . Papa and them are at the fort now. I was allowed to leave only to fetch Mama from Master Taylor's farm."

Raleigh paused again, some of the earlier fear returning to his eyes. "That's where I'm on my way now. He wants me to bring Mama back with me to the fort."

"Bring her to the fort?" Hampton wasn't sure what this meant.

"Yes, as quickly as I can," Raleigh added.

"What can she do there?"

"It's not what she can do. It's what they'll do for us," Raleigh said. "Papa said the Union soldiers will protect us."

Protect *them*? Hampton thought. All this time, there was someone finally sent to protect the poor slave. Raleigh's words fell hard on Hampton's heart. Hampton did not know how the South would stand for this when word got out. The law insured that runaways must be returned to their masters. Hampton worried what would become of Raleigh and his father and the other men if they were wrong and they were sent back to Colonel Mallory; there was only one way to deal with runaways.

"You want to come down to the cabin, and I can fetch you some water?" Hampton asked. "Might do you good to rest awhile."

"No," Raleigh said. "Thank you. I brought my own." He smiled, pointing to an army-issued canteen strapped to his back. Hampton studied it. The weight of it in his hands put more truth and hope in his heart than Raleigh's words could.

Still, he wondered if the Union soldiers could really be trusted. It all seemed so unbelievable. This blessed news did not feel as it should. Hope is not sweet when doubt lingers. Hampton did not want to dash the boy's hopes— he wanted the story to be true.

"Well, you better hurry on along then," Hampton told Raleigh, patting his back.

"Oh, Hampton," Raleigh called back. "You should come too."

"Come to the fort?" Hampton asked, surprising himself at how magnificent the idea sounded in his own voice.

Hampton watched as Raleigh headed off down the road into the night. At the pace he was going, the boy would get to his mother's cabin by daybreak, maybe sooner. Hampton turned back down the path toward his cabin. Ruth was sure to be waiting for him.

He knew what Ruth would say once he told her all he had learned from Raleigh. But how could he tell her what the boy had told him, something not even out of his wildest dreams? Hampton hardly believed it himself, and he knew there was only one way to know for sure.

CHAPTER SIX

Ruth Wilcomb

Even later that night

Walking back to the cabin, Hampton knew what Ruth would say once he told her all he had learned from Raleigh. But how could he tell her what the boy had told him? Hampton was not sure if he even believed Raleigh's story. He would have to go to the fort to see things for himself.

Hampton saw her before she saw him. He called out to her, and they ran to greet each other.

"I thought you were gone," Ruth said, her voice

wavering. "I thought you had made up your mind to leave. I couldn't let myself think you would leave without saying good-bye. When I saw you heading up the road toward the crossroad, and you took off running, I knew you were gone for good." Ruth was in tears.

Hampton held on to her to soften the hurt.

"Have you come back? Does this mean you are giving up that notion of soldiering? Are you going to stay?"

"I don't know," Hampton said. "There is something that I must find out first."

"What of Mister Henry's order?" Her voice shook, and new tears threatened to spill from her eyes, even as Hampton wiped them away. "What will you explain to Mistress, Hampton?"

He hesitated. *Why won't I just do as Raleigh says and go to the fort, tonight?* he asked himself. *What if Raleigh was right, but the Union soldiers went back on their word?* Hampton wouldn't let himself risk his family's safety. He couldn't. There was no way of knowing what would be waiting for his family if he took them all now. No, he would have to find out on his own.

"I . . . I," he started. "I will know what to say to Catherine when the time comes."

Hampton turned to his wife; the grief of losing her boy Joseph was still so new and a heavy weight, a thick cloud surrounding her heart, threatening to smother her. And Hampton's call to leave would only add to that sorrow in her. The deceit and injustice of it was too much.

Henry Warren had sold the boy away to a cotton farmer farther down south to pay the last of his farming debts, barely batting an eye as Ruth wailed on her knees.

He had said that the boy had only been rented out for the cotton harvest. Henry Warren continued his lie, even with the word "Sold" stamped on the center of the receipt for the purchase of slaves.

Everyone for miles around knew Henry Warren to be a man you couldn't call a liar, but he had a way of twisting things, creating empty promises when convenience benefited him.

Hampton had tried to comfort his mourning wife, but Ruth knew Joseph was lost to them forever. And now with war brewing, it would be near impossible to find where the boy was sent, so deep into Confederate territory.

Ruth was grateful to have a husband like Hampton. He was patient and kind. As a free man he could leave and go where he pleased, but he didn't want to do that.

Despite being so learned, he never put on airs. She always felt he loved her, but sometimes she didn't know why. She never felt herself so much of a pretty woman as his first wife, Sara, who had bright skin color with fine features. You could see Hampton and Sara all rolled up in Callie, whom Hampton loved more than the flowers love the sun.

Hampton loved Ruth just as fiercely, just as brightly. He never questioned her silence. He never pushed her to speak until she was ready. When she did speak, he treasured those words like the pearls they were.

Ruth didn't know what she would do if she lost him, too.

Sometimes Ruth felt such turmoil, she did not always know how to express herself, her joy, her pain, her grief, her sorrow, and her understanding of the world. As a small child she had fallen off a water wagon and hit her head against an iron wheel. The accident caused her to lose her voice. For a while she did not speak, long enough that folks wondered if she ever would again.

Ruth did speak, but there was never confidence in the hollow sound of her voice. At times it was difficult just getting her thoughts out in the way she wanted. And so she remained quiet, saying very little or nothing at all, but she listened, and watched, and noticed everything. It made her attuned to the feeling of others.

She sometimes saw her thoughts as tangled pieces of thread in the bottom of her sewing basket.

But there were other times when all of the thoughts would straighten out and coil around like on a spool of thread. Times like that she felt her thoughts were clean as a day after rain. She could hear the words in her mind as straight as pins in cloth, lined up the way she wanted to say them, clear like the sound of a bell.

When she knew what she wanted to say and how she wanted to say it, you could not deter her. She started talking and didn't stop until she had said all there was in her mind to say, even when her voice grew hoarse.

She often wondered if the accident loosened her thinking. There was less holding her together than other folks. And the life of a slave made her unwind more quickly than she should have. But when Joseph was born, or when she married Hampton and embraced Callie as her own, and then when Charles was born, she felt the seams tighten, not as tight as she saw in others, but through it all, the love she felt for her family was enough.

This time it was different. Grief had too strong a hold on her. After Joseph was sold, she began to rise early. She would sit for hours with her arms across her body as if she was trying to hold her whole self together, as if the seams had been ripped out of their stitching. She wished she could pin herself together the way she would pin a dress pattern. There was nothing like that to help her.

One morning as light began to flow in through the tiny window, she looked around her cabin room at what was left of her sleeping family. The seams that held them together were unraveling; she saw it in the slump in Callie's shoulders, in the tone Hampton took with Mister Henry—stifled, tired. Little Charlie had taken another bad cold. The stitching was coming undone in her family, just as it had for her all those years ago. And she could do nothing to stop it. But she knew she *needed* to do something.

"Enough," she finally whispered to the incoming growing light. "Enough."

Hampton and Ruth sat in silence under the dark of the night sky, the stars barely twinkling. They sat together, silent but together.

Callie woke and stumbled to the cabin door in a sleepy stupor.

"What happened?" she asked with eyes barely open.

"Go back to bed," Hampton said gently. He took the child back into the cabin and joined his wife again.

Ruth could see the toll their way of living was taking on her husband. Hampton was free; he could have gone off and left them a long time ago. She had asked him one day why he hadn't left as some men have done. He took her in his arms and asked, "How can I leave the better parts of me behind?"

Ruth decided she had had enough of quiet. Her mind and her thoughts were all straightened out. It was her time to speak, though she did not know exactly what she would say. But when she opened her mouth she found her truth.

She took Hampton's hand in hers.

"It is no one's decision but your own to choose what your living has been and will be, Hampton," she began. "No one knows what path you are on, or where you are going, but God. What you take away with you is what makes you who you are.

"All around the world, everyone has a way of seeing the world for themselves. They are entitled to it. But the job of the life that lives inside of you is for you to take the better and the best and the most that this world can offer. Take it from all the good and beauty you can find, Hampton. Some things in the world are unclean and ugly. Some things are as clean and beautiful as a new day.

"The old world is being burned and torn apart,

Hampton. But beauty is everywhere, even in the ashes. Something beautiful and brand new will rise from it.

"You can never lose when you go looking for the beauty of your life. Let it surround you, and make you what you are meant to be. Let it make you whole. And let no one decide that for you. Plant yourself like a seed to be delivered to the world that is your choosing.

"The brightness of the day is the light you carry inside your heart.

"I must. You must. We all must do what we can to live and to carry on the best we can, so that one day, our children, or their children, will have the right to live free.

"Don't you see, Hampton, this old world is giving way? I feel it—don't you? The war is going to change everything. We must live as if we are planning for the new and better world that is to come."

And then Ruth had said what she needed to say.

The two, husband and his wife, sat and talked long through the rest of the night until there was little more of it.

Before sunrise, a decision was made. Hampton would go to Fortress Monroe to see for himself how things were. This would not warrant saying anything to Catherine Warren, not now. There was nothing to tell, not yet.

Besides, Hampton thought, *I'll return long before supper. I won't even be missed.*

But, he was missed, and in missing him Ruth felt hollow.

• • •

When Callie awoke, the cabin was quiet. The door was open and she could see Mama Ruth. She could smell the smoke from her medicine fire. Callie went to where Little Charlie was sleeping, lay down beside him, and rubbed his back. He opened his eyes, reached for her hand, and smiled. Then the coughing began, and the crying. Callie picked him up and rocked him until he closed his eyes again and went back to sleep; his breathing was labored.

"Mama Ruth," Callie said, giving her a morning hug. "Where is Papa?"

"He'll be back directly."

"Is there anything you need me to do? Mistress needs me to do some housework again today."

"No," she said, nodding, "but thank Elsa for the beef tallow." As she kissed Callie's forehead, she noticed they could look each other in the eye. Her heart swelled at that, and she tucked the warmth of that feeling away for another time.

Ruth kneeled in front of the little fire she had made in the pit outside her cabin door. She was grinding the healing herbs that she had gathered from deep in the woods. She had a small amount of beef tallow. It would have to be enough, but she was still grateful for it.

She sat pounding the stems and the roots of the plant, hoping they would soothe her baby boy. Overnight the fever seemed to have eased a bit, but the baby still took to awful coughing spells that shook his whole body.

Ruth poked and stirred at the small fire—she watched

the sparks and embers rise into the air then go out. Still, she would not let her mind drift.

Ruth mixed the mash of herbs into the grease and heated the mixture long enough for everything to melt and blend together. It needed to cook for a while to draw out the healing properties.

Once it cooled, she rubbed the salve over Little Charlie's body, his neck, and behind his ears. She had enough for a few days. She hoped it would heal the sickness. The rattling cough would not break, it would wake him up and he would cry through the night. Ruth did not know what else she could do to break the awful cough. She swaddled the boy tightly in a piece of cotton she had left over from a quilt she had sewed for her mistress.

After a time, Little Charlie was settled down and sleeping. Ruth listened to the sound of his breathing. It calmed her. She was tired, not just in her body, but her heart and soul were weary of holding so much together for so long.

May 26, 1861

Days drifted from one to the other. Ruth had not heard any word from Hampton; tomorrow would be three days since he left. She would not let herself think the worst of what could have happened to him. She had to live for the children now.

Ruth picked up her basket of piecework. She sat at the open cabin door so she had enough light to see what she was doing. Every now and then a warm breeze or a summer cloud would move across her face.

The warmth of the sun felt so nice on her face. But that did not ease her aching spirit. She thought how good it would be to just close her eyes and let the sun shine on her face—for just a little while. Charlie had not stirred. The remedy seemed to be working. She was thankful for that, very thankful.

She didn't know how long she had been sleeping. She awoke when something, it must have been a cloud, blocked the warmth of the sun from her face. She thought she might be dreaming.

But it *was* Mistress Catherine standing over her, blocking the sun from her. What business did the mistress of the house have here in the Quarters? The mistress barely left the house, and she never came down to the Quarters. If she needed something or someone, she would send another to fetch it or them.

Ruth could not understand why Mistress Catherine had shown up in her dream.

But it was not a dream.

"Ma'am," Ruth said, trying to get quickly to her feet. Now awake, she certainly could not understand what her mistress was doing in the Quarters at her cabin. Ruth stood silent as a stone, unable to pull her thoughts together; she must have slept too deeply.

Three days ago, the horse took fright at something, and it took six hours to set her bones. There are neither mail nor telegrams. People seem to be in waiting for news. So many troops have gone and are still going. Henry...

—*Catherine Wilcomb Warren's diary*

CHAPTER SEVEN

Catherine Wilcomb Warren

May 26, 1861
Later that day

T he mistress considered Ruth for a few moments before she spoke. Catherine did not know exactly what to say to her. She felt she hardly knew her. Even after all these years of dressmaking and dress fitting, the woman was almost a stranger.

Catherine knew Hampton's first wife very well. She had loved Sara, and would never allow herself to get that close again. So Catherine kept a respectable distance, and Henry encouraged it.

"I see you have a nice little garden there," Catherine said, pointing across to the garden patch. It was set off from the rest of the yard by large rocks. "Those look to me like turnips," she said, eyeing the leaves. "Are they tender?"

Ruth was trying as fast as she could to come out of her sleeping stupor. She needed to make sense out of what was before her.

"Did you have any luck with the collards?"

"Oh yes, ma'am. We sent some up to Elsa," Ruth managed to say.

"Yes, I remember the collards. They were good. I think I could have a taste for turnips, if they are tender," the mistress said trying to give Ruth a chance to respond to her. She knew Ruth to be a woman of few words.

Catherine thought she would wait another minute. She was considering whether she would head back up the hill and forget the reason she came down to her cabin.

Then Ruth found her words.

"Ma'am, Mistress? Yes, the turnips are very nice. I had Callie bring some to you to the kitchen door yesterday. She said the door was locked so she knocked; but no one came to answer. She left them there for you, though."

"Yes," Catherine began. "We may not have heard her. I have taken to keeping the house locked up. These are such uncertain times." The woman looked away from Ruth.

"Uncertain," Ruth repeated. "You are welcome to have some. I can have Callie take some back to the house with you. Is Meek still helping Elsa with the cooking for you up there?"

"She is."

"I'll clean them up and have Callie bring them to Elsa."

"That won't be necessary," Catherine said. "I'd be happy to take them with me now. I cannot tell you how much I have had a taste for turnips and cornbread with a bit of salt pork."

"Yes, ma'am," Ruth laughed. "That sounds very tasty indeed."

"Well, the cornbread and the pork are out of the question, but I will be happy to have the turnips."

Ruth quickly put her sewing back on top of the basket. She went across the road to her little garden. "I'll pick you a few nice ones—tender ones," she said, smiling.

"Not too many. I know you have to eat too."

Ruth used her apron to brush off the loose dirt from the turnip roots. "Let me go wash some of the dirt off."

"Never mind," her mistress said. "I can take them like this." Catherine seemed eager to hold the plants whether they were caked with dirt or not, claiming them as hers.

"How is Little Charlie? Callie tells me he has a fever and a bad cough."

"Yes, he does, and I don't know what else. I doctored on him a while ago and finally got him to rest. It seemed to quiet his cough. I thought I could get a little rest for myself just now. Then I woke up and saw you."

"I have a bit of cough syrup here from Elsa's cabinet," Catherine said, reaching for something in the folds of her skirt. She handed the bottle to Ruth. "Keep it. Use it all if you need to."

Ruth took the precious bottle, holding it in both her hands.

"Thank you so much. Thank Elsa for me. I surely appreciate this, Mistress. I'll give him a dose before he sleeps tonight. Maybe that would help him rest through the night."

Catherine fashioned a weak smile as she held the turnips in her arms. She did not seem to mind the dirt on her bodice. "I hope it helps," Mistress Catherine replied.

There was a stillness neither one could fill with words or smiles or gestures. The two women stood facing each other not in judgment but curiosity.

It was somewhat comforting for Ruth to see her husband's face in the face of her mistress, even if some days it frightened her too. Ruth found herself staring at her mistress as if she were some kind of map with signs and a direction post that would help her discover something new.

"It sure is an honor to have you come here," Ruth said, breaking the silence. "But if you had sent word, I would have brought them up to the house for you."

"When we were children," Catherine began, "Nancy, our nurse, would sometimes dress us alike.

"Hampton had so much of the Wilcomb blood in him people who didn't know our family often thought we might be twins. But as you know I am older than Hampton."

Ruth looked at her mistress without saying a word.

"He got the name Hampton from me. I named him for the nearby city of Hampton, Virginia."

Catherine broke her gaze. This talk made her uncomfortable. These kinds of familiar things did not get talked about at all and especially in mixed company, slave to master. Catherine shifted her weight from foot to foot. Suddenly she could not stop herself from speaking, as if the floodgates had opened.

"I was not raised for these kinds of affairs," Catherine said. "I don't think I ever really considered what side of things I stood on. I was taught that this was all men's business. You can imagine that left me ill prepared to cope with the upheaval of what is happening in our lives. There was so much being done. . . ." And then her voice trailed off as if she was poised on the brink. Of what? Catherine didn't know.

"But you tell me, Ruth, what could *one* woman do?"

Catherine seemed to have held on to her thoughts for too long. Now her words stood between the two women, creating a denser forest—a higher wall to climb.

"I love Hampton," Catherine finally said. "You know

we lost my sister, Eloise. Mother, Father are both gone. I never had—" Her voice finally broke.

"Hampton is my only family, he is all I have—my father's only son. But I always felt him to be my brother, even though we only share one parent." She paused and her words gathered weight over Ruth.

"It was hard on Mother. But she had been ill so long. I am glad she did not live long enough to know Hampton because she would have loved him and that would have broken her heart. She had already suffered so much before she died.

"The relations we have between each other . . ." Catherine paused, seeming to consider what she was going to say. And then she began again.

"The relations we have between each other, slave and master, are crude and strange, I will grant you that. Many of us do not question slavery. It is something that we just accept. But I daresay that I do not wholly know how to live in it. It can make you feel that a part of you is all but disappeared or someone else breathes through your lungs, sees through your eyes, speaks your words, and stands in your place entirely." Catherine stood motionless, seeming to try to catch her breath.

"I loved Sara, too," Catherine began again. "I think it grieved me as much when she died as it did Hampton. She was Hampton's wife and so that also made her my sister. I accepted her.

"I was with her and the midwife in the cabin when Callista was born. Sara had talked all along about what the baby's name would be if it were a girl; she loved that she could name her daughter for a cluster of stars," Catherine said, mustering a slight smile.

"When it became clear that—" Catherine's voice broke. She collected herself and continued her story.

"When Sara died, I made her wishes known and *I* named the baby. Hampton was in no shape. He was lost to his grief and his joy—so odd to have so much of both, and all at once.

"I had wanted to send for the doctor, or to take her with me into the house, but Henry would not have it. And when he finally agreed and the doctor arrived . . ." Her words trailed off again. "It made me so sad for us to lose her.

"I'm glad Hampton found favor with you," she said. "I was satisfied that you were a good choice. I could see that in your kindheartedness you would make a good mother to Callie. You had a good temperament and fine dressmaking skills. But there would be nothing I could do should my husband decide to send you away. I told Hampton as much.

"You are a good woman. I know why he loves you and why he married you. But I did warn him about what could have happened. There was nothing I could do about Joseph. I am so very sorry. I have made inquiries, but unless there is a miracle, I fear he is lost to us for good. Everything is so tangled up in this war business."

Catherine stopped abruptly. There was surprise in her face, as if she had not intended to reveal so much, but it gave her relief as well. Ruth did not know how to pin this together in her mind. There had been so much in Catherine's words, and Ruth was unsure of what to make of it all. Finally, her mistress spoke again, worry etched in the lines of her face.

"He's gone . . . ?"

It was less a question, but Ruth still managed to answer. "Yes."

Slave laws were the law of the land. What General Benjamin Butler did in declaring slaves to be contraband was to give the North a legally defined term. Refusing to return the escaped slaves to the Virginia slave owners initiated the process that would later lead to emancipation.

CHAPTER EIGHT

Hampton Wilcomb

May 24, 1861
Daybreak, two days earlier

Hampton loved the coolness of the forest just before sunrise. Slaves often had to use this secret road to get to the river. He used it also, but especially in these uncertain times. Sometimes he would use this path to leave the plantation at night for a swim or to catch fish.

There were times when he would take Callie and Joseph fishing at night, the way his father did when he was a boy. His father had tried to teach him how to catch fish using only his bare hands. His father had said it was a skill to be mastered, but Hampton never felt he would master it. He preferred a fishing pole. But still, he tried. He'd grab hold of a fish, but it would wriggle and wiggle out of his hands. It was Joseph who became the best fish catcher.

Hampton or any slave in his or her right mind never would have walked out in the open in broad daylight anyway. It wasn't safe. Even though so few white men were left behind, they were always on the lookout to pick up a slave—to turn him in for a reward or, even worse now, to ship him off to the battlefield.

Hampton arrived at the fort in good time. He had not thought how he would inquire about Shep, or Frank, or James. He decided to watch awhile before asking around. It was still early, and the world was quiet. He resolved to swim across the river to reach the fort so he would not be noticed.

The cold of the water made him more alert, helping him focus on what was to come next. He needed to confirm all of what Raleigh had said before he could act. He hid himself very well in a thicket of brush.

Before too long, a Confederate officer rode up to the fort. Hampton did not recognize the man right away, but from the way he was dressed, he appeared to be a major at least. No doubt this business was important, likely something to do with his three friends. All of a sudden the gate to the Fortress opened and the General of the Fort rode out on horseback.

The two officers regarded each other.

Neither man would dismount, keeping a proper distance from the other, speaking calmly and in gentlemanly tones to one another. Hampton listened intently as the two men talked. The rebel officer spoke first.

"I am Major John Cary. I am in charge of Colonel Mallory's property," he said. "I have come here as we have been led to believe that three Negroes, property belonging to Colonel Mallory, have escaped within your lines and are being held here."

Major Cary studied the man in blue as he answered back slowly.

"I am Major General Benjamin F. Butler. And it is true. We hold three such persons here."

"And what is your intention for Colonel Mallory's slaves?"

"My intention is that they will remain here at the Fort," Butler said. "Under our protection."

"What about your constitutional obligation to return slave property? And adherence to the laws of the land?" the major asked.

The general smiled.

"Constitutional obligation? Adherence to what law? Of whose land?"

The rebel officer seemed confused.

"It is now my understanding that Virginia no longer adheres to the laws of these United States. You have now seceded from the Union. You are now a foreign country, are you not?"

The general continued slowly.

"Since these three men tell me they were engaged in the construction of artillery batteries for your foreign government, I shall claim them and hold these Negroes as contraband of war."

It is just as Raleigh explained, Hampton thought.

If the general would not send back Colonel Mallory's three slaves, citing Virginia now as a foreign country, then the law no longer stood in Virginia. Virginia had voted to secede, or split from the Union, and was no longer subject to the laws of the Union, the United States.

Hearing this, Hampton abruptly stirred, almost giving himself away. If Hampton's mind had not been made up, it was certainly made up now.

He wanted to run home, gather up his family, and return to the fort immediately. Still, he kept to his hiding place behind the shrubs, trying to prevent his excitement from giving him away.

Hiding there in the bushes reminded him of his childhood with his sisters. The three of them together. Hide and Seek was a favorite game they played. The two girls would hide in places so that they could be easily found. But Hampton always found the best spots where he could stay hidden for hours. He would often grow tired of waiting to be found, and Edward Wilcomb would often find his boy snoozing in a tree, too high for anyone to climb to reach him.

As a child, he spent many a day in hiding, learning

about the secrets of the Wilcomb family and their slaves. Many of the questions he had about his mother and why he could not see her were finally answered.

Catherine always said Hampton had the habit of showing up in places and getting an earful of news. He certainly got an earful today.

When he awoke, the fort was teeming with activity. When things settled down, he would head back home. He could hardly wait to get back to Ruth and take his family with him to the fort.

Hampton did not know how long he had been asleep. He stood up to stretch his legs and felt a churning in his stomach. He realized he had not eaten anything since yesterday, but he did not mind. Soon enough he would be home.

As he stood at the river's edge, the sun seemed brighter and the air fresher. Hampton turned to go on back home to Ruth to share with her what he had learned. He knew when he explained everything she would understand that leaving Belle Hill Farm was exactly the right thing to do.

Something caught his eye. He watched a young soldier on a raft on the river. The soldier seemed to be more of a boy than a soldier. He watched the young fellow for a while. The young man was having trouble turning the raft. It appeared his oar had gotten tangled in some brambles on the river's bottom. Hampton tried to motion to the soldier to slow down, that his raft was about to turn over.

Then, to make matters worse, just before the fellow

went under the water, he hit his head on the side of the raft. Though he wanted to spring into action, Hampton waited to see what the young soldier would do. He hoped the soldier would soon break the surface of the water and take air into his lungs. But the soldier did not appear. Hampton could no longer wait and he jumped into the river. He swam to where the young man had fallen. From the surface of the water he felt around to see if he could find him. Having no luck, Hampton went back under the water. He came up for air, but he had not found the man. He took in a deeper breath, went underwater again, and came back alone.

Finally, Hampton took in one big breath and pulled himself under the water for what seemed a long time. When he broke the water's surface, he felt the soldier's coat and pulled him to shore. The weight of the uniform threatened to drag them both back down, but Hampton was a strong swimmer, even tired and hungry. When they reached the shore, Hampton turned the soldier on his belly. He pumped as much water out of him as he could. By now the sentry soldiers in the fort could see help was needed. Two or three guards were on hand to help; one carried a stretcher. Hampton stood back as the man coughed river water out of his lungs.

"Do you think he'll be okay? I got him out of the water as quickly as I could, but he had gone down pretty deep. He hit his head pretty hard too," Hampton said to one of the guards.

"You think he'll be all right?" Hampton asked again out of concern, expecting the guard to answer.

But instead the fellow who almost drowned suddenly answered. "My head is a whole lot harder than you think. And I am very grateful you were there." Having said his piece, the fellow lost consciousness. The other soldiers moved quickly to his aid.

"I think he'll be all right," the oldest of the guards told Hampton.

"What are you doing here?" another asked. Hampton hardly had time to answer.

"You'll need to come into the fort with us," said the last, standing from his unconscious comrade. "We'd like to ask you some questions. Besides, I am sure when he comes around, he'll want to thank the man who saved him."

And with that, Hampton was taken into the fort.

News of the three slaves, James Townsend, Frank Baker, and Shep Mallory, taken into the fort and not returned to Colonel Mallory spread quickly. Daily many more fugitives arrived at the Union Army fort seeking protection from their slave masters. They were not just young men but women, and the elderly, and families. Some could hardly walk. They may not have understood what the contraband policy at Fort Monroe truly meant, but it satisfied them to know that at least they weren't slaves anymore.

CHAPTER NINE

Callie

May 27, 1861

E very day and several times a day Callie found excuses to go back to the cabin from the Big House. She was checking to see if Papa had returned yet. Mama Ruth answered her the same way each time she asked.

"He should have been home by now," she said, trying to sound as if it didn't matter that she did not know what had happened to him or if he would return. She would only say she prayed that he had not gone to fight in the war and silently worried that something far worse had happened to him. Callie hoped beyond hope that Papa was safe. But then Papa didn't return the next day either, and neither Mama Ruth nor Callie knew where to put the thoughts that floated around in their minds.

That night Callie found her stars twinkling in the sky. She hoped Papa was seeing those same stars and he did not feel that he was lost and alone. She made another wish for his safe return. "Please look down on him. Look after him," she said. "Please bring Papa back home."

And that next day, something wonderful happened.

Two riders came tearing up the road on horseback toward the Quarters. That changed everything. Callie worked in the small garden tending to the plants. At first she could not make sense of what she was seeing. Callie thought she knew she should be scared, but she did not feel especially afraid.

She called for Mama Ruth, but she was busy doctoring on Little Charlie. He had caught another cold and was not feeling well. Callie squinted to see if she could make out who the two men were. One was dressed as a Union soldier. Without Papa or Joseph with them, Callie wondered how she should greet them. But she did not feel fear.

A Union soldier was riding alongside someone she thought she might know. The other man reminded her of Papa, the way he looked when he would ride a horse. He sat up tall and proud. Then the fellow she thought she might know took off his hat and started waving it and hollering at the top of his lungs and calling out her name.

Callie thought that the man waving his hat and yelling looked like Papa. She called to Mama Ruth again. "Please come out here, and quick!"

"Callie, Callie-girl, it's me. It's me—your papa. Fetch Ruth. Fetch your mama. I told you I'd be back!"

It was her papa. He had come home. Something inside of her made her open her mouth wide and she screamed to Mama Ruth. She jumped up and down. Callie could not stop jumping up and down as the joy spilled out from her eyes.

Mama Ruth finally came running. She was carrying Little Charlie in her arms. She had been nursing him day and night. But nothing ever made him feel better for long.

Charlie lay so still in her arms. But when Mama Ruth whispered to him, "It's your papa," and he heard Papa's voice, he reached out his hand to touch Papa. He smiled at Papa up on the horse. Callie could not stop her tears, and she did not want to. They were the happy kind of tears.

With all that had happened, she had forgotten how happiness felt.

Then Papa jumped down off his horse. He grabbed ahold of his family and wrapped them up in his arms, hugging them tight. Callie did not care that she could hardly breathe. But poor little Charlie, she thought. He would have been jumping for joy at seeing Papa again if he were feeling better. They all cried and hugged one another over and over again. After they got finished with all the hugging, Papa said he had come to claim his family. He said he had the right to come and claim them.

Mama Ruth just kept shaking her head and laughing. "Where'd you get that soldier hat?" she asked.

Papa was wearing a blue Union soldier hat. He tipped his hat and put it on Mama Ruth's head. Everybody laughed.

"From this fellow right here," Papa said, and slapped the young white man on his back, which almost knocked him off his feet.

"Forgive my manners," Papa said with a big grin to the Union soldier. "This friendly fellow is Lieutenant Mathew Jessup." The soldier turned a bright shade of red and smiled at Mama Ruth.

"This is my wife, Ruth; my daughter, Callie; and my boy, Little Charlie," Papa said, taking Little Charlie in his arms. Papa carried Little Charlie to the cabin step, sat down, and rocked him.

"How do you do, ma'am?" the soldier said, extending his hand to shake Mama Ruth's hand.

"I'm doing just fine, sir," Mama Ruth said, before turning back to her concern for Little Charlie.

"I can't get the fever to stay down or the cough to go away," she told Papa as she wiped Little Charlie's sweat on her sleeve. "I have done all I can do for him. There is not a doctor around anymore. They all joined the fight. We just have to wait and pray."

"Aw, Charlie boy, it's your papa." Charlie looked up

and put his little thin arm around Papa's neck. "He'll get much better when the army doctor looks at him," he said, smiling at Little Charlie. "You wait and see."

"Army doctor, Hampton?" Mama Ruth said, her eyes wide as the moon.

Papa laughed a big, deep belly laugh with a twinkle in his eye like he did when he thought something was so funny. "Slavery is over for you, for us," he said as he wrapped up his son in his arms again. Mama Ruth steadily shook her head. Callie sat down next to Papa and folded her knees under her dress. She just wanted to be close to him and make up for some of the time she missed him.

"Something new has happened in the world, Ruth," Papa said. "Now we all can be free! And we can get Little Charlie looked at by a doctor, too, at the army fort!"

"What are you talking about? Is the war over?" Mama Ruth asked.

"It might as well be."

She hesitated. "I don't want to be anywhere near to the war. But why would they tend to our boy, Hampton?"

Papa said there was a way to be free on account of he was taken into the Union fortress as contraband of war.

"What does that mean?" Mama asked, bewildered.

"What ever it means, you are no longer a slave," Papa said, hugging her with a big grin.

Mama looked from Papa to Lieutenant Jessup.

"Well, ma'am," the lieutenant began, "what your husband is telling you is all the way right. It's a lot to take in, but that is where things stand right now. The laws of the land do not include Virginia."

Now Callie looked from Papa to Mama Ruth and to the soldier. She did not know all of what was going on, except she liked it, whatever it was. This soldier thought of her father as a friend, and enough of a friend to help them. He kept calling Mama Ruth "ma'am," like she was somebody particular and special, the way a white lady was spoken to around here. Callie sat there rocking back and forth with her hands on her knees.

"Yes, ma'am," the lieutenant said. "I come from a Northern state called Vermont. It's just like I told Hampton, before the war, I had never seen or talked with a Negro and never even considered them to be a friend." Callie almost wished Suse was around to see and hear this young man speak about her father as a true friend.

The lieutenant's face turned red again and he looked down at his boots.

"I joined the army as I saw it was my duty to my country. Then, when Hampton here jumped in the river, risking his life to save me from drowning of my own stupidity, it all changed my heart. I don't know what my family would say, but I consider your husband to be a loyal friend. I will always be in his debt. Because of him, I get to have my birthday in a few weeks," he added, cheeks turning red again. "So I've come here to help your husband bring all of you back to the fort with us where it's safe for you, and you'll be looked after."

Mama Ruth looked to Papa. He knew she would not take one step off the plantation unless she had a full understanding of things at hand. She had a lot of questions she wanted answered. Callie wanted to know too.

Papa took one of his hands holding Little Charlie and rested it on Mama Ruth's shoulder. "Come inside the cabin, Ruth, Callie. Let me tell you everything that has happened and how it is that we are leaving here today. But then you have to promise me we will move quickly!"

They all went into the cabin. Hampton had so much to tell them about meeting Raleigh at the crossroad and everything that he saw and did at the fort and how they could be considered free.

Sitting at her papa's knee, Callie could not believe his words could be true.

CHAPTER TEN

Leaving

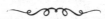

May 27, 1861
Later that day

Callie thought Papa came in like a strong wind to push out the clouds after a heavy rain. Things were moving fast. Callie thought she liked it but she also felt it was too fast to suit her. Papa talked fast too. She especially liked the things he was saying. His plans seemed to have adventure running all the way through them. But they scared her too. She had never left Belle Hill Farm for even a day. And now Papa was saying they were leaving forever. She felt the world was all mixed up and swirling around inside of her even more.

"Ruth," Papa said, "I want you to start packing the things you want to take. I'm going up to the house to speak with Catherine Warren." He paused, and suddenly his voice became very heavy.

"No matter what, she deserves our respect and friendship. She has done right by us. She never broke her promise to us."

Callie became all eyes and ears. This was no dream happening. This was truly real.

"I'll stay behind here and help with your little boy so your wife can pack," Lieutenant Jessup said, reaching for Little Charlie. Papa nodded his head in thanks.

"You come along with me, Callie," he said, taking her hand. "Speak your piece to Suse. I don't know when you'll see her again."

Callie was glad he said that. She guessed she did want to see her and say her farewell, though she didn't really know what she would say to her. She wasn't sure she knew the words to say good-bye to Suse.

Papa knocked at the door.

"Catherine," Papa called to her in his sweet, soft voice. "It's Hampton. Catherine, could I please have a word with you?" Callie had hardly ever heard Papa refer to Mistress by her first name. Papa stepped back off the porch and waited patiently with Callie in the yard.

Moments passed. No one came to the door right away. Papa knocked again. Callie wondered why no one came to the door. She was sure Papa's knock was loud enough. She wondered if Mistress Catherine didn't come to the door because she was feeling as afraid as she was.

What Papa was saying frightened Callie. What he was talking about, freedom, was only spoken about like a far-away dream—a dream that might never come. But this day freedom was finally here. It was hard to believe.

To Callie it was all so confusing. Her head felt dizzy. Her stomach was churning. She felt jumpy inside, but in her heart she felt that same shining light that shone on Papa's face. They were changing their lives forever.

The door opened but Miss Catherine did not open it very wide. When Papa went up to the porch, she stepped outside to speak with him. Callie hoped Suse would be with her, but Miss Catherine was alone. Callie stayed in the yard hoping Suse would see her from the window and come downstairs.

The sun was bright and high now. Callie put her hands up to shield her eyes and looked up to Suse's window. Callie could not see Suse's face, but Callie was sure she was standing there in her window, peering down into the yard. Suse was not timid like her mother. When she pulled back the curtains, Callie waved and motioned that she should come downstairs. She waved at her again, but Suse closed the curtains and did not come out to the yard, either.

Callie wasn't so sure if she wanted to say good-bye forever or just farewell to Suse. Maybe, she decided, it would be nice to have a friendly talk with her. But it was probably too late for that now.

Then Hampton turned to his daughter.

"Go on gather your belongings, Callie," Papa said gently. "Tell your mama I will be there directly."

When Callie got back to the cabin, Little Charlie was still resting on his pallet sleeping peacefully. Mama Ruth had all the blankets spread out on the floor. Lieutenant Jessup was happy to help. Mama was telling him what he could put into a blanket so that it could be tied into a bundle. When Mama Ruth looked up and saw Callie, she smiled. Callie looked around the room that was their cabin.

"It's so empty," she said.

"It's not much," Mama Ruth said to Lieutenant Jessup, "but it is all we have." Then, she spoke to Callie.

"Callie," she said, "I have something for you to pack in your bundle. I have been saving this and holding on to it, waiting for the right time to give you this."

She handed Callie a package wrapped in store-bought paper. There was something soft inside.

"What is it?"

"Open it and see."

"Should I wait or open it now?"

"Yes," Mama Ruth chuckled. "Open it now." Callie quickly untied the string holding the package together.

"It's . . . so pretty," Callie said, smiling and unwrapping the package. "It's calico, blue calico cloth."

"Yes," Mama Ruth said. "I've been saving this cloth for you, my Calico Girl." She smiled a wide smile. "I never knew when I'd get the chance to piece out the dress for you or when you'd be able to wear it."

"How did you get it?" Callie asked.

"A while back, Mistress hired me out to her friend, Mrs. Edwards. And Mistress made me promise that I would do my best to make Mrs. Edwards happy. Mrs. Edwards was very happy with my dressmaking skills. After I finished the sewing for her, she wanted to pay me real money. But Mister Henry did not agree.

"'What can I do for you, then?' she asked me.

"'Of all things,'" I told her, "'I'd like a yard of calico, to make my daughter, Callie, a real dress to wear.' She was a kind woman. She gave me not one yard, but two yards of it as payment for my work. Isn't it beautiful?"

"Oh, Mama," Callie said. "Oh, Mama, Mama, Mama, this is beautiful," she said, hugging her. Callie hugged the cloth and Mama Ruth so tight. She could hardly wait to get out of her itchy slave clothes.

The calico cloth had little blue flowers on a cream-colored background. "I know how much you love this fabric," Mama Ruth said, and she kissed the tear that rolled down Callie's cheek. Then she laughed a little. "Calico Girl," she called her. "As soon as I get a chance I am going to make you the prettiest dress. You'll be proud to wear it. It'll make you feel like you are a brand-new person! There is even enough here to make a bodice, too."

Callie smiled, hugging the cloth. She looked down at her linsey-woolsey. Then she looked at the old party dress Suse had given her.

"Mama? What should I do?"

"Do about what?"

"This dress Suse gave to me." Callie held it up. "I do not want it. I don't know what to do with it, either."

"Don't you want to take it with you?"

"No, Mama," Callie said.

"Then give it to me, Calico Girl. I'll put it in my bundle. My sewing needles can always find a use for an old party dress," she said, laughing. Mama Ruth smiled at Callie and then she started crying.

"Why are you crying?" Callie hugged her.

"Callie," she said. "You keep calling me *Mama*. You didn't call me Mama Ruth. You called me Mama like I was your mama and not another name."

Mama Ruth was so happy. Callie didn't know what to think. She never thought about calling Mama Ruth anything but Mama Ruth. Now that their lives were changing it was as if everything inside her mind was changing and getting free too. So much good was happening. And she had a feeling that so much more was going to keep happening. But things were far from the kind of good that she wanted for her family, all of them.

She wished Joseph could be here with them, and she wished Little Charlie felt well enough to join in the happiness.

"I'm glad to be leaving and going to freedom," Mama Ruth said, sighing and closing up the bundle. "I pray the army doctor can help my little baby."

One of the last things Callie placed into her bundle was the little doll Joseph made for her that night after Calper's Cave. Joseph was good with his hands. Callie didn't know how he could create some of the things he did. The doll was made out of dried corn husks. There was a swatch of pink calico wrapped around it for the body. He attached a twig to the back. The very top of the twig was made into the shape of a star, which hovered over the doll's head.

"This is for you, Callie-girl, so you never get lost again and you will always remember our stars," he had said, hugging her.

The doll was all Callie had left of Joseph except for his old boots, which she would have had to wear when she outgrew her own. One thing for sure, Mister Henry always made sure they had good leather shoes. She took off her boots and placed them in her bundle. She put on Joseph's boots and laced them up. At least his boots would be able to walk into freedom, she thought.

"We should be on our way now," Papa announced, standing in the doorway of the cabin, folding papers and placing them into his shirt pocket.

"Catherine gave me Callie's freedom papers," he said. "I don't know what we need them for now," Papa said. "But I took them anyway."

Callie's heart swelled with excitement!

"Did you talk to her about leaving?" Mama asked.

"Yes," Papa said, nodding. "It is done."

Callie rode on the horse with the lieutenant, while Mama and Little Charlie rode with Papa.

She could not say she understood her feelings. They were leaving the only home she had ever known and they did not ask the master or mistress for their permission. Callie felt that she had slipped out of her own skin.

As they rode off through the gates of Belle Hill Plantation, Callie looked back at the house. Her old life flashed in front of her. She could not help but wonder if this was the life she would truly leave behind. It had been all she ever knew. The Big House of Master and Mistress Warren had always been so full of life and so big and grand. There was always much coming and going. Now the house and the farm looked so small, so hollow and empty, as if there were no life to live there ever again.

With every step of the horses' feet, as the estate became smaller and smaller to her eyes, she prayed and hoped that they were gone from there for good. She was glad to be leaving this place where a person had no choice, no say in his or her life. She thought of poor Joseph, wherever he was, and the other men, who were bought and sold or split apart from everything they loved.

"What do you think of all of this, Miss Callie?" Lieutenant Jessup asked as they rode together on the horse.

At first she thought to say she didn't know. But then she caught the words before they spilled out of her mouth and said, "I want all of us to have a say over our own lives and what we do for the rest of our lives," she told him proudly. "Yes, that is exactly what I want."

PART TWO

The New World Begins

CHAPTER ELEVEN

Fort Monroe, Freedom's Fortress

May 27, 1861
Later that same day

Arriving at the fort, Callie could not believe her eyes. The fort looked like a castle as she had seen in one of Suse's books. But she had never seen a castle that stood on an island like this. The fort looked sturdy and strong. The walls were made of stone. Lieutenant Jessup said the walls were ten feet thick. The walls of the fort looked as if it would never fall down.

"It is a commanding structure—*impenetrable*,"

Lieutenant Jessup said. "It was built to last forever," he added, almost in awe himself.

The fort stood there as if to say, "I was built here to protect all who live inside. I am standing here for a reason and I shall not be moved."

Like a castle, it had a moat. Beyond the moat was another wall as thick as the outside walls. There were small arched windows that served as lookout places. To get inside, a stone-covered walkway led to a door of the fortress. Sentry soldiers with rifles and bayonets stood all around. So much was happening all at once.

To enter the fort, Callie and her family had to dismount from the horses so they could register with the sentry guards. Lieutenant Jessup took the horses in through the gate and the Wilcomb family were counted and listed on the roster. Callie and her family stood at the gate with seven or eight other freedom seekers.

"This is Freedom's Fortress," Callie heard one of the men say to someone.

Callie liked that two of the soldiers knew Papa and were friendly to them.

Once inside the fort, Callie was glad to find Lieutenant Jessup there waiting for them. She could have missed him standing there if he had not called to her papa and waved. Her eyes were so full of looking around. It was nothing anyone could have imagined. Callie had to look at everything twice. There were wagons and mules and soldiers everywhere.

They had to be careful where they walked, since they shared the road with the horses carrying soldiers and mules pulling wagonloads of supplies. All of a sudden, there was a big commotion. A mule bucked and kicked. He toppled over the wagon. Provisions and supplies went everywhere. It startled Callie and she bumped into the lieutenant, almost knocking him over.

"You'll get used to all the noise and commotion," he said, smiling and straightening his hat.

Groups of soldiers were marching this way and that. More soldiers appeared out of nowhere running with bayonets. People moved quickly as if they were hurrying to get things ready for something. Giant cannons were being hauled up to stone towers. There were people who weren't dressed as soldiers drawing pictures of everything happening in the fort. Newspaper people were talking to the soldiers who were standing around. It was hard to imagine that such a place existed so close to Belle Hill Farm.

It felt like a little town inside of a town for soldiers, with so much life going on and so many moving parts. There was even a general store, a tailor shop, and a blacksmith.

Strangers were everywhere: Other families like Callie's were walking around. She could tell some of them had walked a long way to get here; they moved as if they were not sure where to step. There were so many other kinds of people, all walking and talking and working together. But still others walked as if they had grown up living in this fort their whole lives. It was like nothing she had ever seen before.

"Are we going the right way to get to the doctor?" Mama asked. Her face looked worried.

"It's right up ahead," Papa said, pointing toward a brown building.

There was a building at the back of the fortress for the the freedom seekers. Papa and Lieutenant Jessup had a place where they could put their things and sleep. Callie saw many other contrabands who walked about so freely. Some of the men carried shovels, picks, saws, and other tools, going in one direction or another. A group of women were starting to plow up plots of land to plant seeds. They waved and Callie waved back.

"What does all of this mean?" Mama Ruth asked Papa, her eyes wide. She still seemed so nervous after all of this.

"I don't rightly know, Ruth, but we'll see day by day. This is all happening so fast, I don't reckon anybody truly knows. For now, we are free, and have protection," Papa said to Mama Ruth, sounding confident in order to help settle her nerves.

"Protection," Mama said, as if repeating the word would help soothe her. "Will we be at the doctor soon?"

"Yes," Papa said. "We are walking in that direction. I didn't tell you earlier, but I have been hired by the Union Army to be a scout in Lieutenant Jessup's regiment."

"My superiors believe your husband would be a fine addition to my men," Lieutenant Jessup added. "I recommended he be given a position myself." And there was such pride in Papa's face at that.

"And I know the soldiers and officers are in constant need of mending and sewing, Ruth," Papa said.

Callie looked from Papa to Mama. She was still wearing Joseph's boots. He was not here to walk into freedom with them, but it felt right that something of his was on freedmen's grounds.

"The hospital is right up ahead here," Lieutenant Jessup said, pointing.

"You mean we can go in there and get the doctor to help us?" Mama asked.

Lieutenant Jessup looked at Mama and then at me.

"Ma'am, you are free. You are free to choose what you want for yourself and for your family," he said.

"Free to go to school?" Callie said.

"Yes, ma'am." The lieutenant grinned. "Over there is Tyler Villa," he said, pointing to one of the buildings.

"They all look the same," Callie said. "I wonder how anybody can tell which one is which."

"You'll get used to it, Miss Callie," he said. Then he turned to Mama Ruth. "A schoolroom has been provided for the children," Lieutenant Jessup said.

"You mean Little Charlie and I can learn to read and write?" Callie was excited to hear that news.

"Look, Charlie." Callie had to walk behind Papa to see his face. "Look over there," she said, pointing. "That's our schoolhouse. Hurry up and get well, so we can go to school together. We'll be going there to learn when you feel better." But he never lifted his head from Papa's shoulder.

"Go ahead," Lieutenant Jessup told Callie. "You can walk over there right now if you want. No one will stop you." He took her bundle and carried it. Callie looked at Mama and Papa and they both smiled and nodded.

"The teacher is there already. Go meet her," the lieutenant said, smiling.

"A *teacher*?" Callie almost shouted.

"Hampton," Mama began.

"You go on ahead, Callie," Papa said. We need to find the doctor right away so he can take a look at Charlie. The army hospital is right here." He pointed to one of the buildings.

"Shouldn't I go with you?" Callie asked.

"I think you'll like the look of that schoolroom," Lieutenant Jessup said with a smile.

Callie walked quickly to the long building that would be used for the schoolhouse. There was more commotion going on. Soldiers were unloading boxes off a wagon and bringing them into the room.

A woman was there, and Callie was speechless. She had never seen a freed*woman* before; she did not have the worried look in her face as she had seen slaves to have, not being able to be their own selves. The teacher stood tall, and her smile was kind. She smelled clean, like good soap. And she was even wearing a dress with a calico bodice. She was beautiful.

There was a bowl of oranges in the room on the front table. Callie immediately felt hungry. But she felt her spirit lift when she saw her face. She was talking to what looked like another free person, a man.

"Truly, Mary, I don't know how long this will last," the freedman was saying to the teacher. "Every day more and more of our people arrive. We cannot stay on this fort forever."

"It is a start, though," she replied. "That is why they sent for me to come and set up a school," she said, looking toward the door. "And the new people are already here!" she said, gesturing to Callie, who was standing there.

"Well, I will leave you to your organizing," the man said, smiling at her. "I'll see you at the meeting tonight." He tipped his hat to them both and he was out the door.

"Come in," the woman beckoned. "Come in! Are you one of my *scholars*?" she asked, smiling.

"Scholars?" Callie asked. She was not sure of the word the teacher had called her. She had never heard such a word before. She was not so sure if she had even heard her correctly.

"When we open for the weekday schools, will you be one of my scholars? Students," she said. "I do hope you will be one of the students."

"Oh yes, ma'am. I do so plan to be one of your *scholars*, and my little brother, Charlie, too. He is a little sick right now, but I know he'll be ready for schooling very soon. But we both are your new scholars," she said, beaming. "Mama and Papa and I would like that very much."

Her smile grew very wide. Callie thought the freed-woman had the kind of face she always wanted to see.

"Good. My name is Mary S. Peake," she said, extending her hand for Callie to shake it. "What is your name?"

"Callista is my name. But my family calls me Callie," she said, smiling and looking at the teacher's beautiful dress. For some reason Callie didn't feel afraid to talk at all.

"What a beautiful name," the teacher said. At that moment Callie could not help the sound of her stomach growling.

"I was just about to have something to eat. Would you like to have an orange?"

"Oh." Callie hesitated and her mouth watered. She would love to have an orange to eat. As if reading Callie's mind, Mrs. Peake took two oranges from the bowl. She offered one to Callie; the other was for herself.

"Let's sit for a while," she said, smiling.

Mrs. Peake peeled both oranges, setting the peels aside, and placed the orange slices on a small plate. Then she broke each orange into sections.

"Help yourself," Mrs. Peake said. "Do you know what Callista means?" The sweet juice from the orange filled Callie's mouth. She could not remember ever eating an orange as good as this one.

"Callista means something?" Callie said, shaking her head. "Papa never told me that."

"All words, and that includes names, have a meaning," she explained. "And *Callista* means 'most beautiful.'"

"It does?" Callie asked, looking down at herself.

When she did, she saw Joseph's work shoes. Her face grew hot. She wondered about Joseph and where he was. For a moment, Callie's mind drifted. Callie wanted to find her mama and papa. This was all happening too fast.

The freedwoman sat silently. She put her hand on Callie's shoulders.

"Are you free?" she asked.

Callie shifted her feet. "Ma'am?" She let out a quiet sigh. Mrs. Peake lifted Callie's chin so she could meet her gaze. Suse used to do that, but much more harshly.

"Are you free to help right now?" she asked. "There is a good deal of work to do if I am to be ready when the school week starts, Callista."

"Oh yes, ma'am. I *am* free," she replied, saying the word for the very first time. Callie let it keep ringing in her ears. *I am free!*

"Good," she said. "We can start by unpacking the books and placing them on the shelves." She opened each box.

Callie had never seen so many of the same kind of books together before. Suse had a shelf of books in her room, but there were never *this* many.

"Callista, can you read?" Mrs. Peake asked.

"A little," Callie said.

". . . a little?" she repeated.

"Yes," she said, more surely. "I can read."

"Good. That is a good place to start!"

Mrs. Peake showed her where to place the books. Each time she opened a box, she read the book title out loud. There was a *Primary Speller*, a *Primary Arithmetic*, a *Picture History of the United States*, a *The Eclectic First Reader*, and a *Webster's Speller*.

"Do you know what else I like about your name, Callista?" Mary S. Peake asked.

Callie looked up at her from the books in her hands. Mrs. Peake had a very nice smile.

"There is a very old story, called a myth, that tells of a very brave huntress named Callista who was transformed into a bear."

"A bear?" Callie asked.

"Yes, and there is more. She was set into the night sky among the stars that make up the constellation of the Big Dipper."

Callie's face lit up. "I know those stars! That is why Papa keeps telling me to look up at my stars. Papa has told me about them many times. He also told me about my name, but he never explained why my name is in the stars. Now when I get home I will tell him. He'll be glad to know what I learned in school today. And my little brother, Charlie, likes to hear stories too. Is there a star called Charlie?"

"Not that I am aware of," the teacher said, and smiled. "But the name Charles means 'army warrior.'"

"Army warrior," Callie repeated.

"Papa said our mistress made sure I got the name my mama wanted me to have. My mother died before she could name me. But I have a true mother in Mama Ruth."

"Well, it is a beautiful name."

"I like your dress," Callie admitted. "I love calico fabric best. It is so soft."

"Of course you would like calico," she said. Your name is Callie!" They both laughed at her joke. Callie felt so at ease talking with Mrs. Peake. Already she seemed like a very good friend.

"Yes," she said. "Mama sometimes calls me Calico Girl. I have some of the cloth now. Mama is a seamstress, and she says once we are settled here, she will sew me a dress."

"Since you like this fabric so much, perhaps you will become a teacher. We need good teachers. It is not a written rule," she said with a twinkle in her eye, "but most of us teachers wear calico."

CHAPTER TWELVE

Little Charlie

May 30, 1861

Three days later, when Lieutenant Jessup came to fetch Callie from the school, she knew there was trouble. He brought her to her parents, who were at the army hospital. Little Charlie had gotten sick all over again. This time it was worse than before. And there was a new army doctor caring for him.

Mama Ruth said she liked the first doctor who tended to Little Charlie. The new doctor, Doctor Steward, said Little Charlie never really got completely well.

He said Little Charlie needed to stay in the fort's army hospital, where he could watch him closely. Mama would stay the night with him. Doctor Steward said the family could do nothing else but wait and watch.

"There is no sense in saying 'if you had brought him to me sooner,'" the doctor said. "We'll just see what we can do for him and see how he gets through the night." Callie knew Doctor Steward thought it was comforting, but it was not. It made Mama cry even harder.

Little Charlie made it through the night but Doctor Steward said he did not know how many more nights.

The next day was Friday. It rained all day. Little Charlie just could not make it through another night.

Callie was glad for the rain. Many of the people who traveled here in search of freedom had died since arriving at the fortress. When the chaplain came to see Little Charlie, he said nice words and prayers over his body. Papa held on to Mama and Callie. She was on one side, Mama was on his other side.

Because of what he died from, he would have to be buried very quickly. "Disease in this heat can spread very rapidly," Doctor Steward said.

Callie looked at Little Charlie on the hospital bed. It seemed he was too little for the bed. He lay so still. She felt sad and sorry for him. It wasn't the kind of sadness she felt for Joseph. This was different. Little Charlie's body wasn't strong enough to get well. And he was with his family and his family did everything they could.

She cried for Little Charlie because he never had the chance to get big. He never had the chance to go to school to learn. Callie wanted to hug him one last time, but Doctor Steward said not to. He did not want her to catch what Charlie had.

"At least he died free," Callie told Papa. "And he did not have to grow up and be made to feel flat like you say you feel sometimes. The way I sometimes feel. He never has to worry about being sold away from us, like Joseph. I know his little soul is going to heaven and not to the other place."

Papa listened quietly.

Callie was glad that Little Charlie was spared of the bad things this life can bring, but that did not make her happy. She never got the chance to tell him that his name meant "army warrior."

She felt she had to do something. She didn't know what it was but she had to think of something more than just cry. That was all she wanted to do.

While Mama was getting Little Charlie ready, Callie went back to get something out of her bundle. Papa was digging a little hole in the back of the fort. This didn't seem right to Callie either.

Mama had him all wrapped in his old blanket when Papa came to get him. Callie was heartbroken to see her little brother this way. He always was just a jolly little fellow before that awful sickness came upon him.

"Wait, Mama," Callie whispered through her tears.

She removed the blue calico cloth from the brown paper package she held behind her back and handed it to Mama.

"Wrap Little Charlie up in this," Callie said, sniffling. It is better than his rough-feeling blanket. And he liked the color blue as much as I did."

Callie hesitated. She was holding something else behind her back.

"Put my little corn husk doll with him too, Mama—so he won't feel alone without us."

Mama took the doll and the fabric, and they both cried. Mama wrapped Little Charlie in the beautiful little blue flowered cloth and she put the corn husk doll near his heart. It was the only way Callie knew to say good-bye to her little brother.

Later that night, after the rain had stopped, Callie went out to stand at Little Charlie's grave. The sky was clear and the big wide moon shone down. Her stars twinkled overhead. She pretended Little Charlie was right there with her. Callie thought she could almost feel his little hand inside of hers. She looked down at the mound of earth that held him and talked to him.

She pointed up to the sky. "See my stars up there inside the Big Dipper?" she told Little Charlie. "That is the brave huntress who was turned into a bear. She is free to roam the heavens. Callista is her name."

She spoke to Charlie with what was inside her heart, even though what she wanted to say was so hard.

"Do you see those stars, right next to mine?" she asked,

still pointing. "I am naming those stars for you. They will be called Charles, because a brave huntress might need help from an army warrior sometime." And then she told Little Charlie what Papa told her.

"You'll never be lost from me. You'll never be lost from Papa or Mama or Joseph. You'll never be lost from us in the world," she said. Then it felt as if Little Charlie wasn't holding her hand anymore, as if he let her hand go. But she stayed standing there for a little while longer, just looking up at their stars.

CHAPTER THIRTEEN

Mrs. Peake Makes a Visit

June 3, 1861

That next day, and the day after that, Callie did not get out of bed. Something heavy was pressing down on her, and it seemed to all but push the air out of her lungs. She could hardly move. She wondered if she would ever feel any differently. She wondered how Mama and Papa were able to move around and do the necessary things they did.

She could not understand why so many bad things kept coming into their lives, even though now they were something else other than slaves. Callie thought it all had to be her fault for all the bad things she had said about her life as a slave.

"I never took the time to take back those words even after we were no longer at Belle Hill Farm," she told herself.

Her family was closer to freedom than ever. Their lives were not perfect, but Callie felt things were better. She could go to school. She was the teacher's assistant.

She wondered if she was also the reason they lost Joseph. She never, ever said sorry to God, not once. Callie thought it did not seem right that Little Charlie had to pay for her bad behavior too. He never had a chance at life or to read. She thought it all had to be her fault.

"This has to be my punishment," she said to herself. "First Joseph and now losing Little Charlie."

Each night she would cry herself to sleep wondering how Mama could lose so much and keep going. She wondered why Mama was not in the bed next to her crying her eyes out too. Mama had lost both of her natural-born children. Now she only had Callie because she married her papa.

Callie didn't think she wanted to go to school ever again. She didn't think she should even stay at the fort. She wondered if maybe it would be best for her to leave Papa and Mama and go back to Suse and Belle Hill Farm. She knew Suse was sure to be angry with her, but at least she would not bring any worse luck to her papa and especially not Mama, she thought.

That third morning when Callie woke up, all the noises around seemed dull and muffled. She lay on her back and cried looking at the ceiling. She did not hear Papa or Mama tiptoeing and whispering around her as they sometimes did. Outside she heard voices of people going on with their day. She heard soldiers marching. She heard people laughing as they went by and she wondered why anything could be funny at a time like this.

Then she heard someone's footsteps walking up to the door. There was a knock on the door. Callie was too tired to answer it and she hoped they would just go away. The crisp, sharp sound of someone knocking came again and again. Callie thought Mama or Papa would say something to the visitor. The door opened and shut and there were footsteps.

"Hello?" called a woman's voice. "Hello, Callie?" It was not Mama's voice.

Who's there? Callie thought. Her throat felt dry and parched.

"Callie? It's Mrs. Peake."

Mrs. Peake? Callie thought to herself, and her tears started up again. She turned her face to the wall away from her. She did not want Mrs. Peake to see her like this.

"Callie!" Mrs. Peake said, and smiled. She pulled a stool next to Callie's sleeping cot and sat down.

"I've missed you at the school," Mrs. Peake began. Callie could smell the fresh scent of soap on her.

"The children miss you too. They wonder when you

will return to the schoolroom," she said, and paused.

Callie wanted to speak to her friend but she did not know what to say. She didn't know how to say anything. Then Mrs. Peake started rubbing Callie's back and patting her, which made her cry even harder, but Mrs. Peake kept on talking.

"I brought you an orange," Mrs. Peake began again, and started to peel it and break it into sections.

"I have at present a total of thirty-nine scholars for the morning classes. Our lessons are exciting. And our learners are all so eager. They range from five to thirteen years of age. If you were there, you would be number forty. Isn't that a good number for a classroom of scholars?"

The burst of orange fragrance made Callie's mouth water.

"I-I," Callie stammered in a whisper. It was all she could say and she started to cry all over again. All she thought she could do was cry.

Mrs. Peake stood up, put the orange on the stool, and sat next to Callie on her cot.

She patted Callie some more, and Callie cried harder. Then she lifted Callie from the sleeping cot into a sitting position and wrapped the girl in her arms.

"There, there, there, now," she said over and over. "I'm sorry for your family's loss. I am so very sorry," she said, patting her and letting her cry.

"It's hard. These are some hard and terrible times. These are some hard and terrible times for our people.

And these are some hard and terrible times in the world. But I do not know of a time in the world when things were any different.

"You must, we all must do the best we can with these times, Callie, for yourself. For others. For the ones we love and the ones who love us."

Mrs. Peake sat with Callie, holding her until her tears stopped. She turned Callie's face to look at her.

"Sometimes that is all that can be expected of us, to do our best. If this is your best, Callie, then that is good enough for me. Understand? We all have some things in our life that we have lost that tear us apart, that make us feel we cannot go on. But you must go on. There are things that make us sad. Still, you must rise above these things and have the life you are intended to have. Life and the ones we love expect and require this of us."

Callie lay back down and said nothing. Hot, fresh tears ran into her ears.

"I would like very much to have you back in the schoolroom with me. You are a good and eager learner. You can learn to be a wonderful teacher," she said, brushing her hair back from her face. "Calico Girl," Mrs. Peake called her. "Don't rush out of your grief, but do hurry to feel better so that you can come back to the school and start your life again. We need you."

Then Mrs. Peake was quiet for a very long time before she spoke again.

"But now I must be on my way. I must greet the young

adult scholars who will be arriving later this afternoon. Your parents attended the adult session last night. I like your parents very much, Callie, very much indeed."

She patted and hugged Callie one last time before she walked to the door. Callie lay very still. She felt sad, but she did not feel much like crying.

Callie listened to the sound of Mrs. Peake's footsteps as she walked to the door until she could no longer hear them. The scent of the orange made Callie realize how hungry she was. She sat up and put a section of the orange in her mouth. It reminded her of the first time she shared an orange with her teacher. It left a sweet taste with her. And times after that, the two often shared an orange from the big bowl Mrs. Peake kept supplied in the classroom.

This time Callie wanted to say something. Finally, she found the words she wanted to say. And she knew to whom she wanted to say them. She spoke out loud.

"There are so many things in the world that are hard to bear. There is still so much about this world that I do not like, but there are some things I do love: Papa and Mama, Joseph and Little Charlie." Callie hesitated.

"And that Little Charlie is in heaven with You roaming around with my brave stars." She hesitated again. "Oh, and calico, and oranges, and of course, Mrs. Peake."

Callie drifted to sleep and she rested much easier this time. She felt better when she woke. When she got out of bed, she went to wash up and get dressed. But her linsey-woolsey dress was not hanging by the washbasin.

In its place was a shirtwaist dress made of blue calico. It did not have a pattern of flowers on it. It was a deep blue, as blue as the color of a cloudless sky. Around its collar was a thin strip of cream-colored ribbon. It was the most beautiful dress Callie ever saw. It was hard to think that it belonged to her. Looking at it carefully, she could see that it was Mama's stitchwork and no one else's.

Callie wanted to put on the dress right away, but she paused, just for a moment. When she put the dress on, she did it slowly and deliberately. Putting on the dress she felt transformed. And she remembered what Mrs. Peak had told her the day when they first met: "It is an unwritten rule, but most of us teachers wear calico."

Callie smiled inside her brand-new self.

CHAPTER FOURTEEN

Mrs. Mary S. Peake

June 16, 1861

After Little Charlie was buried, Ruth and Hampton were very quiet in their sadness. Hampton was often called away for scouting excursions that had him gone from the fort for days at a time. Ruth used her sewing skills and was always busy mending for the soldiers. Callie felt grateful to have a place like Mrs. Peake's schoolroom to go every day. She studied hard, learned quickly. She wanted to do her best and, most of all, to help Mrs. Peake with the big job she had in front of her.

Callie got to know Mrs. Peake very well. And she decided there was no finer person she had met at the fortress than Mrs. Mary S. Peake. Callie seemed to light up in her company. She was a free woman. Her freedom was not like the kind Papa was given. Mrs. Peake was born free.

The two talked often. Mrs. Peake told Callie of her life. Callie thought she spoke to her of these things so that in a way she could use them to help her live for herself. And though there were many things about Mrs. Peake's life Callie would like to have happened to her, the teacher's life was not without pain, sadness, and great strife.

"I was born in Norfolk, Virginia, in 1823. My mother was a free colored woman. My father was an Englishman. I was sent to Alexandria, Virginia, where my aunt lived. There, I attended school. I remained there for ten years of my life.

"I have attended a colored school taught by a colored woman. And I have attended colored schools taught by white teachers. My last teacher was an Englishman named Mister Nuthall. He taught me until our United States Congress passed a law that closed all colored schools in the city. I was forced to leave the school and return home to my mother in Norfolk, Virginia.

"But while I was at school I did my best to learn everything I could learn, Callie. I was happy to learn and study, learning new things every day. I also learned to sew. This is something your mother and I have in common.

"My belief is that there are many great books. But

there is no book greater than the Bible. Learning Scripture truths that are committed to memory should be part of every educated mind. This, coupled with learning the academics, awakens and develops the heart and mind at once.

"You see, Callie, one never knows how long a time on this beautiful earth we have to live, and we must do the best we can with what we have, and to give to others.

"There is a great difference between the present and the past.

"Just a short year ago, only white children were being educated, but now, look at our roomful of colored children and their beautiful and eager faces soaking up all that they can learn. Times have changed, Callie. And they will continue to change for our people and for the better."

One day Callie asked Mrs. Peake something that she could not find in any of the schoolbooks she read. It had been on her mind since before they came into the fort. Callie was not sure how to ask what she wanted to know in the form of a question. Finally, she found the words and said them to her.

"What does it mean to live and be free?" Callie asked her. "More than just being servant to a master or another person?"

"Come and sit, Callie," Mrs. Peake said, patting the seat beside her. "This is a big question. And it means many things to many different people. Each day, you will find out for yourself in your heart and your mind what it means to you. You will see that you are less of that person who served another, and you are more of yourself who determines her life for herself.

"It may happen gradually, but when it comes, you cannot help but to know it. No one can tell you you are free. You will feel it and know it. You will walk through your life in a way that you never knew you could, and as you do, it will feel right and good for you."

Callie thought she understood only some of what Mrs. Peake was speaking about. Sometimes at night her mind was full of memories that took her back to the days at Belle Hill Farm. It seemed so far away and long ago, but in truth, it was not so. Even now, inside the *impenetrable* fortress, Callie still thought of life as waiting for her freedom. And she remembered the fear she felt for Mama and Papa and Joseph and Little Charlie that lived inside of her.

These conversations with Mrs. Peake were good. It seemed that often when she spoke of these things with her teacher, it was as if the world and all of its moving parts had stopped or slowed down for a moment so that she could put things right, inside of her, inside of her head.

Mrs. Peake and Callie talked often and much. Callie did most of the listening. And then one day, Callie began sharing her thoughts with Mrs. Peake.

"I had been given to Suse. For all of my life, I thought of myself as Suse's property. It was as if she owned the very skin I was in and could do what she wanted with it.

"Now I see I am not that girl anymore. It is as if that skin that covered me had grown too small. I feel I have stepped right out of that skin.

"It was like—like stepping out of linsey-woolsey cloth and putting on my calico dress," Callie said, and sighed as Mrs. Peake listened intently.

"I am a brand-new girl," Callie said. "I am a brave huntress who roams the night and the stars, wearing calico."

CHAPTER FIFTEEN

Susanna Wilcomb Warren

July 2, 1861

Lieutenant Gaines, one of the sentry soldiers, stood in the doorway of the schoolroom. Mrs. Peake cleared her throat to get Callie's attention as she motioned toward the door. The soldier beckoned for Callie to follow him. She had been in such high spirits to see the faces of the children eager to learn, she didn't notice him. This day, she was reading with the primer class. There were seventeen children who showed up this morning.

Lieutenant Gaines was friendly with Callie's family

now after Papa doctored his sick horse, Flyer. Papa said Flyer had eaten too much hay and had colic. When Papa saw that the horse was about to lie down in his stall, Papa stopped him. Papa stayed awake all through the night with Flyer to keep him walking until the colic passed. Lieutenant Gaines was very grateful and beholden to Papa after that.

"That man saved my horse," he had told another soldier.

Callie looked to Mrs. Peake. "Go ahead," the teacher whispered across the room. "I can spare you a while."

Mrs. Peake called to the primers, "Children, come and sit with us."

Callie could only wonder what was wrong now. But the lieutenant seemed to have a chuckle at the corner of his mouth.

"There is someone at the entry gate asking for you, Callie," the lieutenant began. "She seemed harmless enough, I waved her to come on through, but she flatly refused," he whispered to her.

Callie could not imagine anyone asking for her by name. She ran her hand down alongside her dress to straighten out the hem and looked up at the sky. It was growing cloudy. There would be rain for sure. Callie walked alongside the lieutenant as best as she could, to keep up with his long strides.

"I'd say she has a temper. She said she would not set one foot on this enemy soil, and she would not leave until I fetched you. She *is* insistent," he said, chuckling.

Lieutenant Gaines laughed, but Callie could not join him in the joke, for the awful, sinking feeling in her stomach. She could not say directly who this could be, but only one person came to her mind.

"Callie?" Suse queried, "is that you? You look so different than the last time I saw you. Your clothes . . ."

Callie smiled, smoothing down the hem of her dress again.

"Well, you come over here to me, Callie."

It *was* Suse. She motioned for Callie to step through to her side of the entry walkway.

"You come nearer to me," Callie said. Suse came closer but stayed outside the walls of the fort.

"Callie!" Suse cried, reaching out to her. "Mother said you would be here at this awful place. I am so happy to find you," she said, taking Callie's hand.

"How did you get here, Suse? Is there something wrong?" Callie asked, looking around to see who was with her. "Is Miss . . ."—she hesitated—". . . your mother here?"

"Old Ben brought me here in the wagon," she said, pointing. "It's tied up on the other side of the river. He's waiting for me . . . for us. "Oh, Callie." Suse began, trying to fight back tears.

"What's wrong? What has happened?" Callie asked out of concern for the girl.

Suse stared at Callie, whimpering.

Now she must look up at me; her forehead only reaches my nose, Callie thought to herself.

"Won't you come in, Suse? I know the soldiers will let you pass," Callie said, looking at Lieutenant Gaines for confirmation.

"I-I had to come to see you, Callie, is all," she stammered. "I had to come to see you before we leave tonight."

"Leaving? Tonight? Where will you go?"

"Mama and I can't stay here any longer, we won't! We are heading to Kentucky. Papa has family there. Mama wants to go, but leaving will just be so awful!"

"I remember that your father had family there," Callie said, not knowing what else to say.

"Oh, Callie, everything is so mixed up. I have felt so alone. I miss Daddy. Mama misses him too. And I have missed you so much. I miss the way we would sometimes talk all through the night. I wish you would come back with me."

"Oh, Suse," Callie began. "I could never . . ."

"Things happened so fast," Callie said. "And without much warning. It's the war."

"The war," Suse repeated. "It is changing everything. Callie, why did you all leave? You heard Daddy tell Hampton he was supposed to take care of us—and his farm. He wasn't supposed to run off like that!"

"Suse, for many reasons Papa didn't run off. You know Papa is not that kind of man—but he is *only* responsible to his family. He talked with Miss . . . your mama about his plans. Besides, your papa did not have the right to give such an order to a freedman."

For a moment, Suse's temper flared again.

"Now, you do what I say! Get your things—no, forget your things. Come with me as you are. Old Ben is waiting," she said, reaching for Callie's hand.

Callie stepped back into the covered walls away from her.

"Suse, we are no longer slaves or property," she said firmly. "We are freedmen and freedwomen. Because General Butler has taken us into his fort as contraband, I am free to have my own will and determine my own life."

"Contraband!" Suse spat out. "I am sick to death of hearing that word. I know what you call yourself," she sobbed.

"I know what I am, Suse."

"I *own* you!"

"I'm sorry, Suse" was all Callie could think to say.

"Oh, Callie, Callie, Callie. What can we do? Callie, I don't . . . Mama and I . . . we just do not know which way to turn. You know our neighbor Mister Howard, well, his slaves walked off the plantation yesterday, just as big and proud as you please. They gathered up their children and their clothes and walked off.

"Then they called Mrs. Howard to the front porch. Mister Howard isn't there anymore. Like Daddy, he went to help our war effort. Those slaves never would have behaved that way in front of him. They would have never behaved like that.

"They called poor Mrs. Howard out to the front porch as big as you please and simply said, 'We are leaving and you cannot stop us.'

"There are some on the Howard place who stayed behind. But they are still declaring themselves free! They proclaimed they *will* leave only when they are good and ready."

Neither girl knew what to say. Callie looked at Suse. It felt as if she was someone she hardly knew.

"We," Suse began, choking on her words. "We have heard no word about Daddy as of yet." Then she burst into tears again. Callie held on to her while she cried. Callie comforted her as best as she could. Callie knew too well what it felt like to lose someone you love.

The wind was swirling around the two girls both in war and change. It tumbled around them and inside them.

"Come on, Suse." Callie extended her hand. "Won't you at least come inside the covered walkway until the storm passes?"

Suse lost her footing and both girls fell to the ground.

The wind began to blow in large, sweeping gusts. Callie thought it might blow them away. Rain clouds were forming, growing thicker, heavier, and darker.

"It's dark in there," she said.

"It's only the storm," Callie told her. They huddled under the covered area to wait out the storm.

"This is like the night we went to Calper's Cave, without the storm," Suse said, trying to smile.

Callie listened to her. Her mind was moving fast.

"Callie, remember when we went into Calper's Cave together?"

"Yes," Callie said. "But we didn't go in together. You made me go into that cave alone."

Then Callie recounted the painful story to Suse as she lived and remembered it.

"We weren't expecting to be gone for very long, but the dark sneaked up on us. At the beginning, we weren't set on going into the cave at all. We only wanted to holler into the mouth of the cave and run. The plan was to wait long enough to see if what they said was true: If you holler loud enough into the cave, you could wake Old Man Calper's sleeping bones and listen to them rattle. And we said if we did, we would run back home. I knew we would one day talk about this adventure for times to come. I didn't know it would be like this," she told Suse.

"But that is not the way things happened," Callie continued. "Mama Ruth says since Mister Calper died such an awful death there, no one has ever tried to live on the land or farm it. The people around here say the land is cursed and the black-and-white tree proves it.

"I remember that black-and-white tree," Suse added.

"Some folks say that tree is there to teach a lesson about living. But Mama Ruth says she cannot figure out for the life of her exactly what that lesson could be. Sometimes folks like to hide their ignorance by pretending to be wise.

"When we finally remembered it was the cave we wanted to explore, it was already getting dark. We wondered if we should just turn back home.

"Then you said, 'When will we ever get this chance again?'

"So together we decided to go quickly to the mouth of the cave, holler, and run on home.

"By the time we got to the cave, it didn't seem like such a good idea to me anymore. But we both said we had to see it through. I reached for your hand, but you moved it away from me."

Suse shifted her weight.

"No, Callie," Suse said.

But Callie continued her story.

Retelling the painful story seemed to give Callie strength. As each word flowed out of her mouth, it was as if some heavy load she had been hauling were being lifted away, word by word. The rain began to fall all around them, so she took her time and would not leave out one little detail.

"You said, 'You should go in there like we said we would. Won't it be fun for you to see how far you can go? And then, holler out back to me.'

"I told you I didn't think I could do that by myself. 'You come, too,' I pleaded. But you wanted me to go in there alone.

"I had never felt so scared. I held on to a wall of the cave. I stuck my head inside. It was so dark in there; I never knew dark could be that dark. I stepped into the opening and turned my head from side to side. There was nothing to see."

"'Well, you certainly won't find the bones right here!' you teased. 'Keep going, and let me know when you get to the end of the cave.'"

"I remember saying that," Suse admitted.

"You wouldn't listen to reason. I don't know why you wanted me to go into Calper's Cave alone and so badly. You even said you were ordering me to go. I tried everything I could think of to get you to change your mind. I told you I didn't have a torch. 'You won't need a torch to hear bones rattling,' you said. I never knew such fear, Suse, and I hope I never have to feel that way again."

"Why did you go into the cave, Callie? Why did you go if you were so scared of the dark?"

Callie looked at her companion. "I think I was more afraid of you than going into that cavern or what you could do to me."

"Afraid of me?"

"Yes, Suse. I feared you. I was your property, remember? You could do whatever you wanted to me. I was afraid of you. But most of all I feared your papa because it was my job to do what you wanted, to make you happy. And I was more afraid of him because of what he could do to me or the lengths he could go to hurt my family and tear us apart."

"Oh, Callie, Callie. I am so sorry."

"So you see, Suse, this life I am living now, as hard as it is I'm glad I'm a contraband now. You can't make me do anything. You can't tell me what to do. You cannot give me orders against my will anymore."

The two girls sat huddled together to wait out the storm. Now Suse was crying again.

"Oh, Callie, Callie. I watched you as you climbed upon those Union horses and rode away," Suse admitted. "I have been horrible to you. Can you ever forgive me? Please say you will."

Callie had not realized it until this moment but she already had forgiven Suse. Somehow, telling the story to Suse took the pain and the sting of it away and out of her. She felt free of carrying the burden of that awful event.

"I am so sorry," Suse began, and started to cry again. Callie patted her and held on to her while she cried softly.

"But I remembered that you did your best." Suse looked up, surprised, when Callie said that.

"You did go to Papa to let him know I was in the cave alone," Callie said, smiling. Then Suse smiled too.

"I did do that," Suse agreed. "And I am so very sorry."

"Suse," Callie began again. "Maybe this is not good-bye. Maybe things will be different after the war is over."

"Maybe," she said. Then she hesitated. "Mama and I talk about you all. She talks about Hampton most. I know she liked having him as a brother and she misses him. I know that makes you my cousin. I've never had a brother or a sister. And I think I would have liked to have a sister, but sometimes I think cousins are even closer than friends. Cousins are almost like sisters. And who knows, when the war is over we might find another cave that we can explore, and this time we'll explore it together."

The two girls laughed. They sat together until the rain stopped. It was still very windy. The sky began to clear. Callie knew she had to get back to Mrs. Peake and the children. She hoped she didn't think she had forgotten her or them. Both knew Suse had to be getting back home.

"Callie," Suse said, "I better head home. Mama wants to leave tonight, but, with the storm, we may have to wait until the morning."

Suse put her arms around Callie. She hugged her in a way that meant something real was very different and better between them.

"I do not know when we will meet again, but I hope we do. I will not say good-bye, Callie. I will only say fare-well."

The two hugged each other one last time. Suse turned to leave while Callie headed back inside the fort. For now, the girls went their separate paths, their different ways.

In addition to the many who came seeking protection under the contraband declaration, the number of soldiers arriving at Fortress Monroe was growing as well. Military battalions were growing and organizing. The question of whether to accept more of the newly displaced persons or, more importantly, where to put them, loomed larger every day.

CHAPTER SIXTEEN

Mr. and Mrs. Fowle's Idea

July 16, 1861

Mrs. Peake asked Callie to get to school early before all the others. There were some people she wanted Callie to meet. When Callie arrived, Mrs. Peake was not alone. There was a white man and woman in the classroom with her. They seemed very friendly to Mrs. Peake and they seemed happy with the schoolroom. Mrs. Peake was giving a tour of the classroom. They were looking at all of the schoolwork that was around the room.

The three of them were speaking in low tones. Callie hoped they would notice her standing at the door. Callie did not interrupt. She did her best not to listen but she could hear what they were saying.

The man was speaking to Mrs. Peake as if they were friends.

"Mary," he said, "it has already been decided. The fort cannot hold the freedmen much longer."

"Yes," she said. "I know this, but they must not turn them out. They come so eager. They have hoped so much. The children are eager to learn."

"What can be done?" the woman asked.

"At least the school will not close. I have already written to the Missionary Society. More teachers and supplies are being sent."

"We must not let them down," the woman added.

"Some have walked many miles to get here. There is hardly enough room for the people who are already here. More and more stream in and continue to come," Mrs. Peake said, and then she noticed Callie.

"Callie, you are here. Welcome! Come in." Mrs. Peake smiled and reached out to hold Callie's hand. "Callie, I'm so happy you are here. These are my dear friends and neighbors Mr. and Mrs. Fowle."

"Do come in," Mr. Fowle greeted her, smiling.

"Let me shake your hand," Mrs. Fowle said. "I have heard a great deal of good things about you, young lady."

"Yes, ma'am," Callie said, smiling and feeling a little

out of place. "I am happy to make your acquaintance." Callie took a glance at Mrs. Peake. She smiled back at Callie and nodded her head so that she could feel at ease.

"Now, let me get right to the point," Mr. Fowle began. "Mary, um, Mrs. Peake, tells us what a good student you are. She tells us how quickly you learn and how willing you are to help others. That is fine and commendable."

Callie smiled a broad smile as her face began to feel warm. Mr. Fowle continued talking.

"We have the money and the means to send a young scholar such as yourself to school. It would mean that you would have to move away from your parents. You would live at the boarding school in my home state of Massachusetts."

"Have you heard of Massachusetts?" Mrs. Fowle asked, smiling.

"Yes, ma'am," Callie said, also trying to smile while looking at Mrs. Peake.

"Mrs. Peake tells me you have the makings of an excellent teacher. And we could always use another good and excellent teacher. Do you agree, Mrs. Peake?"

"Yes, Callie. I do agree," Mrs. Peake chimed in. "I think this would be a wonderful opportunity for you and your family."

"Do you mean Mama and Papa will come with me?"

"No, Callie. The schooling is just for you. Your mother and father have their lives here in Virginia. They told me they have both found work here at the fort."

"Yes, ma'am. Mama is working as a seamstress and Papa works as a scout for the army post, and he helps with the horses," she added eagerly.

"So you see, Callie, that just leaves you," Mrs. Peake said.

"Yes, but I work with you. You said I am a good helper," Callie started.

"Yes, Callie. But you will see there will always be so much work to be done. Your getting an education means that you will be helping me so much more."

"What about Mama and Papa?" Callie asked.

Mrs. Fowle had been quiet. Here is where she spoke.

"Callie, Mrs. Peake introduced us to your parents last night when they came to the evening adult school. They said they liked the idea of your getting a formal education and felt this is a wonderful opportunity for you. They said they would discuss it with you when you came home but the decision is completely up to you and your family," Mrs. Fowle said, smiling.

Callie thought Mrs. Fowle had a kind-sounding voice.

Now Callie was quiet. She did not know where to fix her gaze. Suddenly, Mrs. Peake gave her a hug. And when she hugged her, Callie whispered into her ear.

"What did she say?" Mrs. Fowle asked, excited.

"You tell them your answer, Callie!" Mrs. Peake hugged her.

"Yes," Callie admitted happily. "Thank you so very much for your generosity and your faith in me."

Then she turned to Mr. Fowle.

"Yes, Mr. Fowle, I would like very much to go to school in Massachusetts."

"That's the spirit! That is what I wanted to hear." He laughed. Then he turned back to Mrs. Peake. "Now, Mary, I am on my way and we will make plans together about our newest scholar," he said, and then he and his wife were out the door.

The children were beginning to come into the classroom. The lessons would start soon.

"I do not understand, Mrs. Peake." Callie started to cry.

"There is nothing more to understand, Callie, other than this: Mr. Rollins Fowle is a neighbor of mine. I have known of him many years and of his good works. He is a man who is very kind to colored people," Mrs. Peake said, drying Callie's happy tears.

"Frequently he has bought slaves who were in danger of being sold into bad hands and given them their freedom.

"He is also known for sending a student to school in the North to be educated. He has chosen you this time, Callie, and I agree with his choice. You are a very intelligent and deserving young woman."

Callie was happy to hear these words, in spite of everything. In spite of losing Joseph, the war, and losing Little Charlie, there were so many good things happening at the same time.

"Our people need so much," Mrs. Peake continued. "We need teachers to teach our people to read and to

write. Our people need to be educated for these times, and for all of eternity. And we also have a responsibility to teach our children the right habits of living and the true principles of life.

"So, you see, Callie. Mr. Fowle is not just helping you. He is helping so many others who are yet to come."

When Callie got home for her midday meal, Mama and Papa were waiting for her. They saw the look on her face. They looked like they were holding on to a happy secret that would burst out any moment.

"What answer did you give to the Fowles?" Mama asked.

Callie hesitated.

"She said yes!" Papa said, and laughed out loud. "She said yes!" Then he gave Mama a big hug.

Callie ran to them. She wrapped her arms around Mama's shoulders and looked into her eyes. They could all see how tall she had grown. Then Papa hugged them both.

Callie went through the rest of the day feeling mixed up with happy and sad thoughts at the same time. She admitted to herself that she had never considered living one day in the world away from Mama and Papa.

That night sleep did not come easily. Callie listened to the sound of Mama's and Papa's breathing. The happenings of the day ran through her mind, keeping her awake. She

thought about having to go away from Mama and Papa. She did not want to leave them behind. She did so want to go to school, but she didn't know how to say good-bye.

Callie remembered what Papa said about how as a freedman he could never leave his family behind. And what he said stayed on her mind.

Then she remembered that Mrs. Peake had done has much in order to go to school. She thought about that and realized that Papa leaving them was different from her setting out to go to school.

Finally, she told herself, *Those were different times. In these days, in this time, we are all free.* That cleared her mind and she could sleep.

So much was different at the fort. Things were always in a state of adjustment and movement. One morning shortly after Mr. and Mrs. Fowle's visit, Mrs. Peake had announced to her students that change would come to the fort, and it would be fast. There was no more room inside the walls for the new contraband who continued to arrive. The conditions were very crowded.

CHAPTER SEVENTEEN

Lieutenant Mathew Jessup

July 29, 1861

Steadily more people continued to seek refuge within the walls of Fortress Monroe. These new people who came set up tents and makeshift houses outside on the grounds of the fort, where they had the protection of the Union Army.

On her way to the schoolroom early one morning Callie saw Lieutenant Jessup. He waved to her and Callie waved back. She had not seen him in many days.

"Callie! Good morning," he said. "Where are you off to so early?"

"I have chores to do in our schoolroom before the children come to class," she explained.

"Do you like the school?" he asked.

"Oh yes, I like it very much. It is the best thing for me," she said. "I love learning and I love helping others learn." Then she told him about her good news of going to school in the North and her hopes to become a teacher.

"That is very good news, Callie," he said. "I know you will make a very good teacher. And I know your parents are proud of you."

"Where are you off to so early this morning?" Callie asked him.

"We ship out soon. I'm going to the post office, and I wanted to mail this letter to my parents before I leave," he explained. "Have you ever received a letter or sent a letter to anyone, Callie?"

"No," Callie said, shaking her head.

"Well, get ready for it because when you go away, I'm sure if your parents are like my parents, they will want to hear from you often, maybe even every day."

Callie began to feel uneasy again about going away from Papa and Mama.

"Have you ever seen a letter, Callie?"

"I have seen letters written to Mistress Catherine or Mister Henry, but I never noticed them much."

"Well, let me show you. I'm happy to show you my letter to my parents because I wrote to them about your papa and how he saved my life."

Then Lieutenant Jessup opened up his letter and read it to her.

First Vermont Volunteers
July 29, 1861
Fortress Monroe, Virginia
Dearest Father, Mother, and Sisters,
It has been some time since I wrote to you. I am well and in good health and good spirits. I have been in Virginia some time and on this day, because of the help I received from a Negro, I turn twenty years of age. I will not say I miss you as that will cause all of our hearts to ache and I have a job to do. We all have jobs to do.

There is not much opportunity to write, but I felt I had to take time to pen these few words to you as much is happening and I want you to know what is in my heart before I embark for the battleground. We are preparing for battle. The battlewagons are in sight. I wonder how everything will fit together.

This is all beyond my understanding. But I suppose that is why we are here, which almost seems like a foreign country and not part of the United States. Life is the same here, but it is still so very different.

I will tell you of a bit of a mishap. I took a tumble

into the James River, hitting my head in the process. Had
it not been for Hampton, a Negro, who happened to be
standing along the riverside, I am sure I would not be
sitting here right now writing this letter to you. He risked
his own life to save me. I am indebted to him for my life.
I feel he is a lifelong friend. And Father, if you knew him,
you would find him to be most fine and gentlemanly in
manner.

He is a freedman. As you know I am here in this war
to support our government, but I declare when I set out as
a soldier I did not factor in the human element.

It is most distressing to hear stories of what his family
and his people have endured. What little he tells me I feel
as though I am living out of the pages of the Bible, worse
than when Pharaoh refused to let God's people go. But
these Southern pharaohs would be quick to tell you that
they are in fact following God's law as said so in the
Bible. But I do not think so. They do more to follow their
greed.

I recall the scandal caused in our town when Aunt
Bennett became divorced from her husband, James, for
her infidelity. Someone in our congregation joked that she
should be stoned as says so in the Bible.

And Father, I remember your voice of reason that
spoke about how the Bible is to be interpreted for the
times that we live in now. Perhaps the Exodus story of
the Egyptians was also to teach modern man how not to
live: how not to treat a fellow human being created in the

likeness and image of God. The question of slavery and its
effects is so big and vast; it causes the individual person to
act so severely and cruelly to his fellow man.

I pray the war ends and we are united soon. Write to
me soon. Do please tell Ludie when I return we shall go
fishing and I will catch the bigger fish.

Your loving son and brother,
Mathew

"That's a nice letter, that's a real nice letter," Callie told him. "It sounds like they are not far away from you at all and you are just talking to them."

"That's exactly what letter writing is like," he chuckled. "And that's a good way to think about it."

Callie liked hearing Lieutenant Jessup's letter to his family. Mostly she liked the nice things he said about Papa and what Papa did for him. She was happy Papa had a friend in him.

"My home state of Vermont is right next to Massachusetts, the next state north."

"Next door, that sounds like neighbors," Callie teased.

"Vermont is a beautiful place. I hope you'll get some free time from your schooling to travel there," he said. "Do you worry much about being away from your family?"

Callie hesitated at first. "Yes," she said. "A little." She sighed. "I admit I feel a little queasy about it. If I think about it for too long, my head starts to spin."

"That's normal and natural, Callie. But, well, think of

it like this: You will meet new people. If I had not left Vermont, I would never have known your papa. And that reminds me, you will not be *so* alone. You know of someone in the Jessup family who lives in Vermont."

"Thinking of it that way," Callie said, "I guess that makes it a little better." She smiled.

During the first week of August 1861, so that the city of Hampton, Virginia, would not fall into the hands of the enemy, the rebels burned their homes and the town in its entirety to the ground. Few buildings remained standing. Hampton, Virginia, was left a city of charred remains.

CHAPTER EIGHTEEN

Chloe

August 8, 1861

Another new student entered the school. She was part of a family of five. They had arrived only two days ago from the city of Hampton, Virginia.

When Callie got to school that morning, Mrs. Peake was speaking with the girl and her mother. She heard Mrs. Peake say she agreed with her mother that the schooling would do her daughter very well.

The girl seemed very shy. She was ten years old, but her mother said she was small for her age. Callie smiled at her but she would not meet anyone's gaze. She kept her eyes cast downward and looked at her hands.

As the other children entered the room, the girl kept moving farther and farther away from them and to the seats that were closer to the door.

As Mrs. Peake started the class, she took the girl's hand and helped her find a seat.

"Today," she said, "Callie will do the Scripture reading." She turned the pages to the Bible verse she wanted her to read.

Callie held the book open. She cleared her throat and began to read, listening to the words as her voice filled the room.

"That was very good, Callie," she said.

She placed the Bible back on her table. Callie went to her seat. Then Mrs. Peake turned to the class.

"What do you think the words mean?" she asked the children. "What wisdom will you take away from the Scripture reading this morning?"

Discussion began at once. Everyone who wanted to speak was given a chance. Mrs. Peake encouraged some of the others to say a few words.

When everyone who wanted to speak had a chance, Mrs. Peake looked at the timid girl.

"Now, children, we have a new student today. I want you all to meet Chloe," Mrs. Peake said, and everyone turned their attention to her.

"Good morning, Chloe," they all said in a practiced unison.

"Now, Chloe, what would you like to tell us about yourself?" Mrs. Peake asked. And then she sat down and waited for the girl to stand.

Chloe did not say anything at first. She looked around at each of the children. And then she stood and began her story.

"I do not remember much to say," she began, and trailed off. Mrs. Peake nodded her head and smiled at Chloe. She began again.

"Lucy Union is not my mother," she said, speaking directly to Mrs. Peake. "But I will call her Mother as her other daughters do. They will attend the afternoon class for the older students. My mother died two days ago in the army hospital," she said, pointing in the general direction of the hospital building. Callie looked to where she pointed. She knew the building very well.

"My mother and I left our plantation farm on our own. But she was very sick when we left. None of the others came with us from the old place," she said, and paused.

"We walked and walked. One day my mother said she was too sick and could not go any farther. She fell down to the ground.

"I would not leave her alone.

"Then a woman and man and their family of girls passed us on the road. The woman told us her name was

Lucy Union and her husband's name was Clarke Union. The father lifted my mother and put her on our cart. They brought us to this place with them. Then they brought my mother to the hospital.

"When Lucy Union came back to the hospital to find out about us, they told her that my mother died. She asked the hospital people if she could adopt me. I don't know what they said to her, but I am grateful to be here in this place," Chloe said, and then she looked down again at her hands, which were folded in her lap.

Chloe finally looked up and fixed her gaze on Mrs. Peake. Tears were flowing out of Chloe's eyes. And then, one by one, each student went up to Chloe and hugged her. Mrs. Peake did as well before the day's lesson would go on any further.

After class was over Callie went up to the new girl and shook her hand.

"I am pleased to make your acquaintance," Callie said. She did not know Mrs. Peake was watching them from her desk, very pleased with what was going on.

"I am the teacher's assistant. I will be happy to help you practice your lessons and Scripture reading. I am glad you are here."

Chloe smiled and gave Callie a hug. It was the same kind of hug she remembered Suse had given her.

The crowding situation at Fortress Monroe forced many con-traband to set up their families in large tent cities outside of the walls of the fort and in what remained of Hampton, Virginia. The conditions were cramped and worse than what some suffered inside the fort. Some former slaves who could write would even appeal to their former masters to allow them to return to their previous homes.

CHAPTER NINETEEN

Farewell

August 10, 1861

Mrs. Peake asked the scholars to return to the adult evening school with their parents. That night the room was filled to the rafters.

"I know you will all have questions," she said. "But please hear me out. I will tell you everything."

Then she explained what most of the parents already knew. The fort could no longer hold them. And because of the overcrowding, it was necessary to move the school outside of the fort too.

"Our schoolroom door will not close!" she said firmly. "We will open many other schools for our children to attend. I have been in contact with the Missionary Society in Washington, DC. They will be sending more teachers Monday."

Some parents clapped at hearing this news. Many more had questions for Mrs. Peake to answer.

"Before we end tonight, I will tell you what the children and I have planned. We will put on a pageant for the officers and soldiers as a way of saying thank you for their help. The children will sing, read verses from the Bible, and recite from memory."

The parents were very pleased with Mrs. Peake's idea.

When Callie and her family got back to their barracks, Papa wasn't ready to go inside just yet. It wasn't very dark.

"Let's sit on the porch for a while." The early August wind was warm and breezy. Callie thought it was nice to sit on the porch with Mama and Papa. Papa was staring out at the night like he was looking for something to say while Mama worked on stitching buttons on a dress. Then Chloe and her new mother walked past.

"I came to see you, Callie," Chloe said. "I came to say good-bye, because you're leaving tomorrow and I'm feeling a little low."

"Why?" Callie ask her.

"My best friend is going away and I don't know when I will see her again."

"I'll write letters to you if you write back," Callie said with a smile.

"I never had a reason to write a letter before, but I promise to learn how and I will," Chloe replied, giggling.

Chloe was looking at what Mama Ruth was sewing. Her eyes grew big.

"Are you going to wear *that* dress in school?" Chloe pointed. "It sure is fancy for a school dress," she added.

"Which one?" Callie asked.

"That green one," Chloe said.

It was Suse's old party dress.

"Look," Mama Ruth said, holding up the dress in front of her. "I did some finishing things to this one, too. It looks good as new, doesn't it?"

"Yes, it does," Mrs. Union said, smiling.

"It's beautiful," Chloe said.

"Do you like it that much?" Callie asked.

"Oh, yes indeed. I could never dream of wearing something so fancy and beautiful," Chloe said.

"Why don't you wear it now?" Callie said, looking at Mama.

"Oh, may I?" Chloe asked Mama, and then she looked at Mrs. Union, who nodded.

Chloe put on the dress on top of the one she was wearing. She came into the center of the porch and, under the bright moonlight, twirled all around in front of them. The skirt spread out into a beautiful green circle. It was as if Callie had never noticed before, or maybe she thought she didn't want to notice it, but it was a beautiful dress.

As Callie remembered, Suse did love wearing that dress and brushing her hands past the skirt of it as she was walking. It made a swishing sound.

"Now I will just need to tuck it in here and over here for you," Mama said to Chloe as she pinched together each side of the dress around the neck. "Then it will fit you perfectly." Mama smiled.

"It seems like it was made for you," Callie said, smiling to her new friend.

The dress seemed to make her so happy.

"I plan to become a teacher one day," Callie announced. "And though it is not a written rule, many teachers wear calico. I am more of a Calico Girl myself," she said, smiling to Mama and giving her the best hug. Mama hugged her back and laughed.

"You stand here a minute," Mama told Chloe. "Let me size the dress for you." She placed a pin here and there and then helped Chloe step out of the dress.

"We'd better be heading home," Mrs. Union said. Callie waved good-bye to Chloe and her mother.

Now night was coming on. The moon looked wide and awake. Callie could tell Papa had something important he needed to say. She was glad Papa wanted to talk because she was feeling happy, but she was also feeling a little uneasy. She wanted to hear what Papa wanted to say. He had been quiet for most of the night.

"The word 'bittersweet' describes how I feel," he said in a funny kind of voice that sounded like it was hard for him to get his words out right. Mama put down her sewing.

"There are some things I'm happy about and at the same time, those same things make me feel kind of sad," he said, looking at Mama. "It's what you call bittersweet."

Callie knew what Papa meant.

Then Papa turned and looked at her.

"Most of all, tonight I feel a bittersweetness about our Calico Girl here," he said, putting his arm around Callie.

"I spoke with Mrs. Fowle, and she tells me you will have to write a letter home at least once a week," Mama said, smiling.

"That'll be good," said Papa. "I'll be happy to hear about how you're getting along."

"Yes, Papa," Callie said. "I will. And you'll write back?"

"Yes, yes, yes," Mama answered, laughing.

"When you come home, we'll have to call you Calico Teacher!"

"Calico Teacher," Mama repeated. "That sounds pretty good to me!" And they all laughed. But Mama laughed hardest.

Then they all got quiet again as if the wind blew away all of the words they each wanted to say.

"I suppose we ought to go to bed soon," Papa said. "The morning is going to be a busy one, and it will come soon enough. Mrs. Fowle will be taking you on your big trip."

"I know," Callie said. "And everything will be all right," she told him, taking hold of his hand.

"Even though I will be busy learning I *will not* let myself feel how far away I am from my family. And if I do, I will remember what you told me. I could never be lost from you or Mama. When I look up and see my stars in the Big Dipper, I can never be lost. I will remember that the North and the South are under the same stars where my freedom lies. My freedom is in my stars."

AFTERWORD

While this book is a work of fiction, it was inspired by people who lived and had an active role in these true historical incidents. One such person is Mary S. Peake. Though Peake lived and taught in the city of Hampton, Virginia, during the time that my novel takes place, I have borrowed from her life and likeness to place her in her position at Fort Monroe at the time of my novel.

Peake was known to be a thoughtful person of a calm and even temper. She acquired a good English education. All during her life she had been fearlessly engaged in secretly instructing both children and adults in her home, which at the time was in violation of her state's slave law. Peake showed great strength and fortitude and she worked tirelessly. She had strong religious convictions.

Reverend Lewis Lockwood of the American Missionary Association was sent to Hampton, Virginia, in its first missionary endeavor of the war. A teacher was needed to educate the new freedmen and their children who were now under the protection of Fortress Monroe.

Peake was trained as a teacher. This request allowed her to teach freely with permission sanctioned by the United States government. It was a day and a time she had prayed for for many years.

The AMA hired Mary as the first teacher for the freedmen at Fort Monroe, but unlike this novel, Mary never taught on the grounds of the fort. She taught in the open air under an oak tree in the city of Hampton. Also, she did not hold her first class until September 17, 1861, and for the purposes of this story, I have her teaching in July. She saw the children as very eager learners, as were their parents.

When the school opened, she counted six children the first day. But by the end of the week, the number doubled to twelve. Some accounts say she taught as many as fifty children during the day, and twenty adults in the evening.

Peake's mission as a teacher was to educate for the times in which her pupils lived and for the future. She wrote in her journal, "We want to get wisdom. That is all we need. Let us get that, and we are made for time and eternity." She used her knowledge to find ways to waken the developing minds and hearts in her students.

Peake probably taught a total of three months. She died on February 22, 1862, of complications from tuberculosis. Her tombstone reads: *Mary S. Peake: The First Teacher of the Freedmen at Fortress Monroe, Virginia.*

BIBLIOGRAPHY

Digitally Archived Print Sources

Butler, Benjamin F. "The Slave Question: Letter from Major-Gen. Butler on the Treatment of Fugitive Slaves." *New York Times*, August 6, 1861. Accessed February 18, 2015. http://www.nytimes.com/1861/08/06/news/slave-question-letter-major-gen-butler-treatment-fugitive-slaves.html.

Goodheart, Adam. "How Slavery Really Ended in America." *New York Times Magazine*, April 3, 2011, MM40. Accessed October 28, 2014. http://mobile.nytimes.com/2011/04/03/magazine/mag-03CivilWar-t.html?referrer=&_r=2.

Klein, Gil. "Slavery, Freedom, and Fort Monroe." Advisory Council on History Preservation. Accessed November 25, 2015. http://www.achp.gov/fort_monroe_final_story.pdf.

"Letter from Miss. F. W. Perkins," January 4, 1865, in *The Freedmen's Record*, vol. 1, no. 2 (February 1865), 20. See more at http://www.mesdajournal.org/2012/slave-cloth-clothing-slaves-craftsmanship-commerce-industry/#footnote66.

Lockwood, Lewis C. Rev. *Mary S. Peake, The Colored Teacher at Fortress Monroe*. Boston: American Tract Society, 1862. The Guttenberg Project. Release date: March 4, 2007. Accessed July 5, 2015. http://www.gutenberg.org/files/20744/20744-h/20744-h.htm.

Sellers, John R. *Civil War Manuscripts: A Guide to Collections in the Manuscript Division of the Library of Congress*. 1986. http://lcweb2.loc.gov/service/gdc/scd0001/2004/20040324001cw/20040324001cw.pdf

"Hampton Archive: The Burning of Hampton: 'It seemed as if hell itself had broken loose . . .'" *Daily Press*, August 3, 1997. http://www.dailypress.com/news/hampton/hampton400/dp-hampton400-archive-civil-war-fire-story.html.

"Letter from Miss F. W. Perkins," January 4, 1865, in *The Freedmen's Record*, vol. 1, no. 2 (February 1865), 20. Accessed November 25, 2014. See more at: http://www.mesdajournal.org/2012/slave-cloth-clothing-slaves-craftsmanship-commerce-industry/#footnote66.

"The Opening of the War." *New York Times*, April 22, 1861. Accessed October 28, 2014. http://www.nytimes.com/1861/04/22/news/the-opening-of-the-war.html.

"We was free. Just like that, we was free." National Humanities Center Resource Toolbox. The Making of African American Identity: Vol. 1, 1500–1865. National Humanities Center, 2009. Accessed March 2, 2015. http://nationalhumanitiescenter.org/pds/maai/emancipation/text7/emancipationwpa.pdf and nationalhumanitiescenter.org/pds/maai/index.htm, specifically Identity #7: Soldiers; Emancipation #5–7: Civil War I & II (Slaves and Soldiers, Emancipation: 1864–1865).

INTERNET RESOURCES

African American Odyssey. Abolition, Anti-Slavery Movements, and the Rise of the Sectional Controversy, "Fugitive Slave Law." N.p. n.d. Accessed November 25, 2015. https://memory.loc.gov/ammem/aaohtml/exhibit/aopart3b.html.

"American Experience: Reconstruction: The Second Civil War: Access to Learning." Accessed November 25, 2014. http://www.pbs.org/wbgh/amex/reconstruction/schools/sf_postwar.html.

"Civil War Timeline: Gettysburg National Military Park" (US National Park Service). Accessed May 25, 2016. https://www.nps.gov/gett/learn/historyculture/civil-war-timeline.htm.

http://www.virginiaplaces.org/military/fortmonroe.html.

http://www.dailypress.com/news/hampton/hampton400/dp-hampton400-archive-civil-war-fire-story.html.

"The Contraband at Fortress Monroe." *New York Times*, July 20, 1861. Accessed October 28, 2014. http://usslave.blogspot.com/2011/03/contraband-at-fortress-monroe.html?m=1.

"Fort Monroe Military Base." Accessed November 27, 2015. http://www.virginiaplaces.org/military/fortmonroe.html.

Lockwood, Lewis C. *Mary S. Peake: The Colored Teacher at Fortress Monroe*, http://www.gutenberg.org/ebooks/20744?msg= welcome_stranger.

"The Slave Question: Letter from Major-General Butler on the Treatment of Slaves," *New York Times*, July 30, 1861, http:// www.nytimes.com/1861/08/06/news/slave-question-letter-major-gen-butler-treatment-fugitive-slaves.html.

"The Opening of the War," *New York Times*, April 22, 1861, http://www.nytimes.com/1861/04/22/news/the-opening-of-the-war.html.

"Tombstone of Mary S. Peake." The American Missionary Association Photographs, 1839–1954. Tulane University Digital Library, New Orleans, Louisiana. Accessed July 3, 2016. https:// digitallibrary.tulane.edu/islandora/object/tulane%3A544.

Field Experience

Visit to Fort Monroe Casement Museum, May 2015. http://www.fmauthority.com/visit/casemate-museum/

ACKNOWLEDGMENTS

Support is something none of us can do without. I must acknowledge the following people who sustained me through this new and exciting process. First, I'd like to thank Mary S. Peake, whose unwavering spirit and tireless devotion to educating "her people" inspired me to follow the truth of this little-known incident in history and to tell this story. Being a teacher myself, I felt a kindred spirit with her. I hope she would be proud to read these pages and what I have written here. Also, a sincere thank-you to Adam Goodheart, whose article, "How Slavery Really Ended in America," appeared in the *New York Times Magazine*, April 3, 2011, and is the genesis of this book. I would also like to thank Fortress Monroe Casemate Museum for making me feel welcome at this historic site as I did my research. A heartfelt and a hearty thank-you to Paula Wiseman, wise woman and editor extraordinaire, for your faith in me; to Nancy Gallt, my literary agent, who has been a solid anchor and cheerleader for me; and to my loving and dear friends, whom I confided in for this project: Claudette Giles, for your long hours and tireless devotion; Darwin Walton, who enlivened my spirit and my heart; Kathryn Sapoznick, whose sharp and witty intellect kept me ever moving toward my goal, and Bonnie Guerra, whose clear and honest thinking and encouragement I could not do without. Thanks also to Margaret Hutson, for letting me borrow that wonderful little cabin by the river; Eloise Greenfield, for her light and her laughter; Lisa Vitali, who really is not only a crackerjack English teacher but also a *total* rock star; Marcy Emberger, a dear friend and writing educator; to my wonderful and loving son, Matthew Harold, who is consistent in his confidence and support of me, reminding me to remember my truth; and to my dear and loving daughter, Jessica Harold, whose valuable insights, comments, and crisp thinking keep me grounded but ever reaching for the stars.

ABOUT THE AUTHOR

Jerdine Nolen is the beloved author of many award-winning books, including *Big Jabe*; *Thunder Rose*, a Coretta Scott King Illustrator Honor Book; and *Hewitt Anderson's Great Big Life*, a Bank Street Best Book of the Year; all illustrated by Kadir Nelson. She is also the author of *Eliza's Freedom Road*, illustrated by Shadra Strickland, which was an ALA/YALSA Best Fiction for Young Adults nominee; *Raising Dragons*, illustrated by Elise Primavera, which received the Christopher Award; and *Harvey Potter's Balloon Farm*, illustrated by Mark Buehner, which won the Kentucky Bluegrass Award. Her other books include *Plantzilla*, illustrated by David Catrow, which was a Book Sense 76 Selection, and *Irene's Wish*, illustrated by AG Ford, which *Kirkus Reviews* called "delightful and memorable" in a starred review. Ms. Nolen is an educator and lives in Ellicott City, Maryland.